“Howdy, mister,” [illegible] Tulip's drawl.

“You shore do look like a big city feller. What be yore name?”

“James Robert Prince III,” he answered, bowing slightly. “At your service, Tulip,” he murmured, smiling handsomely.

This man was certainly sure of himself, she thought. He needs to be brought down a peg, and I'm just the one to do it. She looked longingly into his lean features, and shyly reached out to touch his cheek and touch his moustache. She almost snatched her hand away when she felt a flash of electricity between them.

“You shore is purty, mister,” she drawled audaciously, turning her head to wink at the crowd. “Yore jist about the purtiest thang ever I seed. I reckon I jist might ask my pappy to git you fer me,” she said, licking her lips with only half-acted hunger.

James stepped forward, and slid his finger down her nose to graze her full parted lips. “I doubt your pappy's intervention would be necessary, Tulip.”

“Well, Jimmy Bob,” she began, needing to take back the upper hand in their scene, “my Granny Bloom would think yore a *prince* of a feller fer me.” She giggled before continuing, “But you don't strike me as a regular businessman, Jimmy Bob. No siree, you looks more to me like a hunter . . . but I can't rightly decide ifen you hunts the four-legged or the two-legged variety,” she pondered.

“It all depends on which is in season, Ms. Bloom,” he drawled in response. “And if my perceptions are correct, by tonight it will be open season on two-legged mountain gals. . . .”

WHAT ARE *LOVESWEPT* ROMANCES?

They are stories of true romance and touching emotion. We believe those two very important ingredients are constants in our highly sensual and very believable stories in the *LOVESWEPT* line. Our goal is to give you, the reader, stories of consistently high quality that may sometimes make you laugh, sometimes make you cry, but are always fresh and creative and contain many delightful surprises within their pages.

Most romance fans read an enormous number of books. Those they truly love, they keep. Others may be traded with friends and soon forgotten. We hope that each *LOVESWEPT* romance will be a treasure—a "keeper." We will always try to publish

LOVE STORIES YOU'LL NEVER FORGET
BY AUTHORS YOU'LL ALWAYS REMEMBER

The Editors

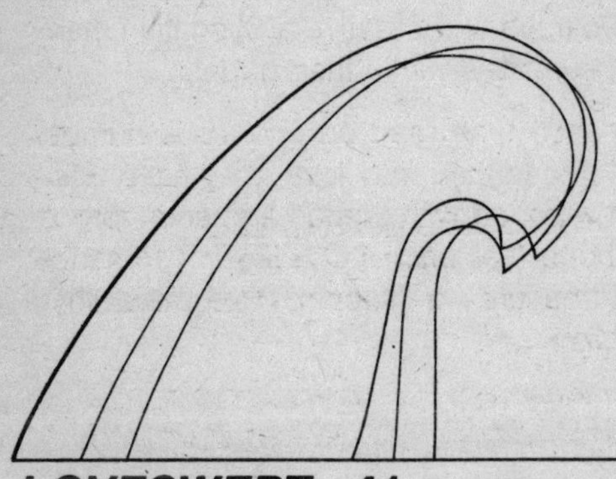

LOVESWEPT • 41

Joan Bramsch

The Sophisticated Mountain Gal

BANTAM BOOKS • TORONTO • NEW YORK • LONDON • SYDNEY

To my Bill

THE SOPHISTICATED MOUNTAIN GAL
A Bantam Book / April 1984

LOVESWEPT and the wave device are trademarks of Bantam Books, Inc.

ISBN 0-553-21656-2

Published simultaneously in the United States and Canada

Bantam Books are published by Bantam Books, Inc. Its trademark, consisting of the words "Bantam Books" and the portrayal of a rooster, is Registered in U.S. Patent and Trademark Office and in other countries. Marca Registrada. Bantam Books, Inc., 666 Fifth Avenue, New York, New York 10103.

PRINTED IN THE UNITED STATES OF AMERICA

O 0 9 8 7 6 5 4 3 2 1

One

Crissy secretly observed the newcomer. He stood at the edge of the circle of tourists she was regaling with a humorous word-picture of life in the Ozark Mountains. After several months in her official capacity as Silver Dollar City's storyteller, she still felt a deep satisfaction when she heard the appreciative chuckles and outright laughter at her down-home tales. In just seven days her job would be over, because the amusement center closed for the season. She'd miss playing her mountain-gal character, Tulip Bloom. So now, with added zest, she continued to spar verbally with her audience and make all of them feel "to home" with amusing stories describing her fictional relatives and kinfolk.

She leaned toward a woman about her age and, using a stage whisper, she inquired, "You shore you ain't kin to the Bloom clan, gal? I swar, you shorely remind me of my cousin, twice removed, Bessie Bloom. Yes, siree, her pappy done shot ten men afore she were fifteen, account of their a-mor-rous intentions! Then one day, she jist up and disappeared with a travelin' man, and we ain't heerd hide nor hair from her since. You plumb shore you was birthed and raised in Kansas City, gal?" All the woman did was giggle and blush furiously at being singled out.

Crissy tilted her head to one side, giving her bouncy black curls a shake that sent tiny shock waves to her precariously perched tattered straw hat with a red tulip growing out of its crown. The gold of her dark brown, heavily fringed eyes danced with merriment as she worked her way around the group, telling one story after another. Her appealing vitality was only enhanced by painted-on freckles sprinkled liberally across her pert upturned nose and round pink cheeks. Her mountain gal costume was winsome and fetching; she was glad it was still comfortable under the Indian summer sun. The top was what she called her "Daisy Mae" blouse—white, with large purple polka dots. Its oversized short puffed sleeves and scoop neckline were attractive, but certainly not daring. The dark green homespun prairie skirt brushed the tops of her heavy clodhoppers.

"Got to ware good sturdy boots ifen you want to outsmart them copperheads," she would tell people who questioned her footwear.

Within a few minutes she'd circled to stand before the stranger. Quickly she sized him up—a practice at which she had become rather astute, and one she thoroughly enjoyed. This man was definitely *not* an ordinary tourist. His well-tailored, three-piece dark suit and light blue dress shirt told her he was a businessman; the expensive silk tie around his collar told her he was a successful one. He was ruggedly attractive, too. About six feet tall or a shade more, he looked as though he might be in his late thirties. His provocative, cobalt-blue eyes sent shivers down her spine when they locked with hers. Was he laughing *at* her or *with* her, she wondered. A light breeze ruffled his medium brown, thick, wavy hair; the September sunlight filtering through the trees glinted off natural streaks of gold.

She was suddenly and vividly aware of his forceful virility.

In her role of Tulip she could be as outspoken as she wanted to be. She continued to grin drunkenly at him. His thick moustache twitched slightly when he tried to suppress the smile playing at the corners of his wide, sensuous mouth. Finally he could not contain it, and when he smiled at her, his eyes lit up and deep dimples appeared as if by magic in his lean, tanned cheeks. How those dimples complemented the cleft in his well-defined chin! She allowed her mouth to gape open in theatrical adulation, but her heart told her with its double-time hammering that it wasn't all an act. He was something else!

At once she decided to go into her flirting routine, sure that the rest of the crowd would enjoy her antics. Sidling up close to his tall, straight frame, she purred enticingly, "Howdy, mister. You shore do look like a big-city feller. Where does you hail from?"

He seemed to enjoy being part of her little act. "I'm from New York City, Ms. Bloom," he answered, his deep voice even, but his clear eyes sparkling with challenge. Her training in speech and theater made her admire his dulcet tones.

She sighed audibly, and gushed, "You kin call me Tulip, mister. What be yore name?"

"James Robert Prince III," he answered, bowing slightly and simultaneously reaching into his vest pocket. "My card," he added, handing her an engraved and thick piece of cream-colored paper. "At your service . . . Tulip," he murmured, smiling handsomely.

She sighed again, this time in earnest, but no one knew, except perhaps the man with whom she was parrying. His eyes grew a shade darker when their fingers touched electrically. Oh, this man was sure of himself, she thought. Needed to be brought down a peg or two, though . . . and she was just the one to do it! She looked with longing at his lean features. Shyly she reached out to stroke his cheek and touch his thick moustache. She almost snatched her hand away when she felt again that chemical reaction. "You shore is purty, mister," she drooled audaciously, turning her head to wink broadly at the chuckling crowd around her. "Yore jist about the purtiest thang ever I seed. I reckon I jist might ask my pappy to git you fer me," she said, licking her lips with only half-feigned hunger.

Before she could continue, he took a step forward and slid his strong forefinger down her ski-jump nose, gently grazing her full, parted lips until he settled on her chin. "I doubt your pappy's intervention would be necessary, Tulip," he said, playing his part to the hilt.

Now, Crissy knew that many tourists were thwarted actors, and she could never be sure how her improvisational skits were going to turn out. But this man's thespian skills were more professional than any other visitor's so far, and at the moment she wasn't all that sure he was *acting*! Take control again, she ordered herself.

"Well, Jimmy Bob," she began, noting with relish how he winced at her blatant nickname for him, "my Granny Bloom would think yore a *prince* of a feller fer me." She giggled with the rest of the group when he raised an eyebrow at her broad pun of his fine, aristocratic name. "But you don't strike me as a businessman, Jimmy Bob. No, siree, you looks more to me like a hunter . . . but I can't rightly decide ifen you hunts the four-legged or two-legged variety of critter." Her jab at his inflated ego was hidden behind an innocent expression. Head cocked flirtatiously, her forefinger pressed against her rosy cheek, she pretended to ponder.

The esteemed Mr. Prince had complete control of his features when he answered in a serious tone, "It all depends on which is in season, Ms. Bloom. If my perceptions are correct, by tonight it will be open season on two-legged mountain gals," he drawled. His comment was heavy with sexual innuendo. "Have dinner with me," he ordered softly, unmindful of the surprised looks on the faces of the strangers encircling them.

"Pappy wouldn't 'low it, Jimmy Bob," she shot back, her eyes narrowing. "Remember my cousin Bessie and her travelin' man," she warned, stepping back into the center of the group and immediately catching everyone's interest with a long-winded story about a citified hunter who used a bird mule. She had the crowd howling with her frozen-statue caricature of a pointing mule. Just as the story ended, everyone turned when the crowd heard a man calling to her from the small stage nearby.

"Tulip! Tulip Bloom!" the man called in his mountain twang. "It's time fer our show, gal."

Crissy excused herself and ran gaily over to the stage and climbed the three steps to the large wooden platform where two men waited for her. Both were dressed in tattered bib overalls with faded blue work shirts and the ever-popular battered straw hats and clodhopper boots. The man who had called her was clanging a huge triangle with a hammer, sending out an ear-splitting announcement of their intentions. "Yo'all come over here and set yo-self down. We's fixin' to entertain you'uns," he bellowed.

Soon the heavy, hand-hewn log benches were filled, and out of the corner of her eye Crissy saw that the unlikely tourist, Mr. Prince, had taken a seat near the front and to the side. His clear blue gaze still held a challenge for Crissy as she walked about the stage, setting up props and waving to the crowd. When it was time for their opening number, she hoisted her unfashionable boot up on the rim of a washtub bull fiddle and began plunking away. One of her partners took up a time-worn banjo, the other a washboard, and the thimbles on his hand beat out a wild rhythm to match the other two. Soon they were warmed up for a rowdy rendition of "When the Sun Don't Set on Bald Mountain, I'll Be Comin' Back to You."

Crissy was the MC, and stepped up to the microphone. "Howdee, folks. I'm Tulip Bloom. This here's my brother Jesse," she went on, pointing with her thumb over her shoulder at the gangling, shy youth at her side. "And this here's my brother Jake," she added, turning to grin at her fifty-year-old partner, who wore a bushy, gray-flecked beard. "They's *twins*, you know," she informed the audience. Hoots and hollers were the response.

"Jake was born first. We never hurries *anything* in the mountains," she declared drolly, waiting with precise timing to go on. "Jake, here, jist looks older," she explained. "He runs moonshine, and he's had enuf close calls with the revenooers to age him twenty years. Jesse, here, jist drinks the stuff, so's he gits younger lookin' every day!" She laughed.

The show moved right along, and, as usual, Crissy's timing was perfect as she fed lines to the two men. They, in turn, gave her the center stage for her storytelling. But part of Crissy's attention was focused on James Robert Prince III. His eyes didn't leave her throughout the performance. The challenge was still there, and she felt drawn to him.

She split the air with a mountain yell, and her face glowed. "Well, gosh o' mighty, folks, I's jist spotted some kinfolk," she said, leaving the stage to plop herself onto Prince's lap. She didn't count on his arms snaking around her waist to hold her tightly in his steel embrace, threatening to cut off her circulation. When she dared to glance at his face, his eyes told her she was going to have to pay a heavy price for making him the butt of her humor. She tried to get up, but he held her fast.

For a moment she almost panicked. But then one of her partners shouted from the stage. "Hey, Tulip, why ain't you givin' our couzin the regular Ozark Mountain greetin' fer kinfolk?"

She looked the man straight in the eyes and burst out nervously, "Becuz he ain't no *kissin'* couzin!"

His deep laugh of appreciation rumbled in his chest. "Don't let that stop you, Tulip," he returned smoothly, shocking her to her toes. When he released her and she could breathe again, he hissed out of hearing from the nearby patrons, "Have dinner with me."

She shook her head sternly and scurried away back to the stage like a flushed rabbit. She took a great gulp of air and went into the closing, which was a foot-stomping, loud-singing, down-home dance number. When it was over, the three performers bowed to the audience and waved, shouting, "Yo'all come back, hear?" When the last member of the audience had left, the team reset the props for the next show and quietly congratulated one another on the good performance.

It was Crissy's break time, and she longed for a big, cool lemonade. She strode along the pathway toward the cold-drink stand, unaware that she was being followed, until she felt strong fingers at her elbow. She knew who it was before she looked around. Keep it light, she warned herself.

"Well, ifen it ain't Jimmy Bob," she enthused. "Yo'all will have to 'scuse me right now, mister. I'm on my break, and I got a powerful thirst," she declared, smiling brightly but trying to pull away from his insistent hold.

Without pausing in his stride, he returned her smile, rather wickedly, Crissy thought. "Good! I'll join you."

She shrugged her shoulders, unable to control the nervous tremors down her legs. This is ridiculous, she scolded herself. You're acting like a silly teenager, and what's worse—you started it! They arrived at the lemonade stand, and she insisted on paying for the drinks, saying, "I owe you that much after all my joshin'." She continued to use her mountain twang, feeling that somehow it was a defense.

"What do you do when you're not Tulip Bloom?" He guided her to a nearby bench and seated her at the corner. When he sat beside her she was effectively trapped between the shrubbery and his hard, warm thigh.

"I teach . . . up in the mountains," she told him hesitantly, deciding she didn't want this man, particularly, to know she taught classes in theater and speech in the high school in Springfield.

She often enjoyed dating interesting men whom she met in this job, but she was always careful to remain a mystery to them. Five years ago she'd almost been raped by a man she thought she knew and could trust. That one terrifying experience—and in her own home—had made her paranoid about guarding her privacy and the exact location of her isolated mountain cabin. Her friends and neighbors knew what had happened, and never gave out information about her to anyone, particularly strangers. Yes, the trusting little country bumpkin had been forced to grow up overnight, but, fortunately, that one bad apple hadn't put her off the whole barrel . . . she had just learned to be very careful and wary of outsiders. And the way she planned any meetings, she was totally safe, always designating a public restaurant, to which she could drive her own car and leave when she wished.

She glanced shyly up into the stranger's face, noting that his eyes were revealing his awareness that she chose to give very sketchy details of her personal life. "What do you do?" she asked, trying hard to sound sure of herself.

"Didn't you look at my card?"

She dug into the deep side pocket of her long skirt and extracted his slightly bent business card, reading aloud. "Prince Toys and Games, Branson, Missouri. James R. Prince III, President." Her eyes darkened as she turned to face him. "You said you was from New York City," she challenged. "This, here, says you has a company right in town."

"I am from New York," he explained, "but I resigned my position at an ad agency there, and I've set up a new manufacturing company here. It's been a dream of mine for some years, and now it's finally a reality." He went on to tell her his company made authentic wooden toys and games from another era. "Old-fashioned and sturdy," he enlarged. "There's too much plastic junk on the market, and I mean to change all that. Children should have toys that spark their imagination." He explained that he had taken over a large plant and remodeled the interior for his operation, which now employed over one hundred people year around. As he told her, Crissy remembered reading about it in the weekly Branson *Herald*.

The business had been started four months ago, he told her, and his appearance at Silver Dollar City was prompted by a meeting he had had with its buyers to insure big orders for next season. "It was a good meeting," he ended, his features unreadable.

Jumping to conclusions and ready to defend her mountain heritage, she rejoined curtly, "We ain't like the characters out of *Deliverance*!" Did he think he could come here and make a killing from some ignorant Ozark folks?

He met her defiant glare with steady blue eyes. "My dear Ms. Bloom, I never thought that for one minute," he said firmly. "The directors here are fine business people. I would never treat them in a condescending manner. They have more integrity than many other business people I could name. Besides," he added, "we understand one another. We want to do business together, and they never hide behind their charming mountain drawl with me. I'm proud to say they know I'm not a big-city shyster, so there's no need to put on an act." He looked at her with hooded eyes. A faint lift of one eyebrow signaled his piqued curiosity. "Now, I wonder, Tulip, why you're hiding behind *your* mountain character."

She had to continue her charade; he was moving too fast for her. "Why, shucks, Mr. Prince, sir. I's jist a country gal, and yore sweepin' me right offen my feet," she gushed, unable to meet his direct gaze, which turned silently to ice.

"I seriously doubt that. What's your name . . . when you're not working here?" he asked, picking up her hand and gently massaging the pounding pulse point at her wrist. "After all, you know who I am now," he murmured.

"My name is Crissy Brant," she answered, just as softly, beginning to feel again the hot flush from their physical chemistry.

He repeated her name as if trying it out for authenticity. "Yes, I'd say you're a Crissy, with your bouncing curls and great sense of humor. Well, now, Crissy Brant," he continued, still stroking her wrist and playing his fingers along hers, "I'll ask you properly. Will you have dinner with me this evening?"

"Are you married?" she shot back, careful to watch for any quickly hidden guilt in his eyes. They held none.

"No . . . and never have been. Are you?"

She shook her head. She wasn't able to stop the dark shadow that momentarily swept across her painted features. He saw it, though, asking, "And have you ever been?"

She swallowed hard. "A long time ago," she answered quietly. "My husband was killed in Southeast Asia. We only had two months together before he shipped out," she said, not knowing why she felt she could share even this small part of her painful memories with this man. "I've been a widow for almost nine years."

He cursed softly under his breath, surprising her with his leashed emotions. "You must have been a baby!" he exclaimed. "I'm sorry to bring up such unpleasant memories," he said with genuine warmth. And he continued to hold her hand.

"I was eighteen," she said, falling into silence as she recalled the fun she and Eddy had had all through school and right up until he was sent overseas. She had known him all her life, and it had seemed perfectly natural to become his wife. But she *had* been very young, and readily admitted to herself that the love they shared was more like puppy love than the deep, abiding flame of passion she now believed a mature man and woman could share. Perhaps they might have grown into that sort of relationship . . . if there had been time, but he was gone before his twentieth birthday, and she had pulled herself together and gone on with her life.

Because she had been an honor student in high school, she was able to get into a work-study program and obtained a small scholarship to New York's City College, where she received her teaching degree in theater and speech. When she returned, she carved out a part-time position at the high school in Springfield from which she had graduated, and was happily involved with her talented students.

Yes, she was happy, and she had gone on with her life. Yet, she felt she was missing something . . . *someone* to belong to, even though she dated often. She went out with local friends and with interesting or affluent executives in Chicago and New York and St. Louis, where she did her freelance assignments as a multi-voiced talent for radio commercials. No one knew about these jobs except those with whom she worked and her best friend, Katie, and they were sworn to secrecy to protect her privacy. She also went by another name—Belle Grady—which had been her married name.

She was that determined never to give another man the opportunity to catch her with her guard down. By nature, she was a giving, loving person and, although she had learned to measure the worth of a man, she was not willing to take chances.

She shook herself, coming back to the present when the man beside her quietly took her empty plastic glass from her nerveless fingers. "Oh, I'm sorry," she apologized lamely.

"Just have dinner with me, Crissy," he replied, taking her hands and bringing her to her feet before him. "I want to know you better," he said, persuasively, his eyes dwelling on her full mouth for just an instant.

Crissy felt his animal magnetism threaten to invade her own body. Her mind sent out the alarm—self-preservation! She threw herself back into her role and replied brightly, "Why, Mr. Prince, I declare. Yore a persistent cuss, ain't you?" His raised eyebrow was her only reply as he patiently waited for her answer. His strong fingers still held her hands. Finally she turned a deaf ear to her survival instinct, and accepted his invitation. "All righty, we'll have vittles together this evenin'. Does you think you kin find the Wooden Nickle restaurant? It's a mite offen the main drag," she warned, grinning. "We don't want yo'all to git lost in them thar hills."

"I'll find it," he answered without smiling. "Will I need a new pair of bib overalls?" he asked, deadpan.

She chuckled in appreciation. The man has a sense of humor, she thought delightedly. "Nope! This here's a fancy place, where you kin git all gussied up, Mr. Prince. Eight o'clock, then?"

Again he ran his fingertip down her pert nose, pausing longer this time at her warm lips. His eyes spoke more words than she was willing to read at the moment. "Eight is fine, Crissy . . . and the name is James." His deep voice caused her stomach to do a flip-flop.

"But Jimmy Bob is so cute," she teased, giddily looking forward to the evening ahead. She scurried away from his light hold. "Gotta go now. See you at the Wooden Nickle."

"Wait! How will I be able to recognize you in street clothes?"

She turned around, skipping backwards. "I'll be wearin' somethin' red," she yelled, tweaking the red tulip on her hat. "It's my trademark. But, don't you worry none, Mr. Prince . . . I'll find *you*!"

She turned and ran back to work but not before she heard him roar, "*James!*"

Two

Crissy's summer home was a hand-hewn log cabin hidden from the road by acres of thick woods from which her grandpa had cut the timbers for his bride's honeymoon cottage.

Crissy's growing-up years had centered around this home. She was brought here when she was barely twelve years old, after her mother's unexpected and untimely death. Granny had raised her from that time, and Crissy had many fond memories of their good times together. When her grandmother had passed on, her beloved and only grandchild had been in college, barely making it home in time to say good-bye. And Crissy still missed her . . . terribly. It was only in the last few years, during her summer storytelling job at the amusement park, that she was able to give life once more to her granny's ribald humor and witty viewpoint of human nature—Granny Brant had become Granny Bloom!

Crissy got out of her little red car and walked up the slight incline to the front porch steps. She never failed to marvel at this little home. It was perched on the hill, needing little upkeep and laughing at the attack of weather and the ravages of time. She entered the one room, furnished with a small table and four chairs, made by her grandfather. There was, too, a comfortable old brown mohair sofa and chair, which Granny had gotten back in 1936 by bartering twenty-seven quart jars of peach preserves, eighteen bushels of homegrown green beans, and an even hundred quarts of garden-fresh strawberries. These two pieces of furniture sat on a large, hand-braided rag rug, made by Granny from worn-out clothes and household linen. And although two kerosene Aladdin lamps still sat in the cupboard by the sink for emergencies, the house was now "electrified," as Granny had been fond of saying. As a surprise for her ninetieth birthday, Crissy had gotten the art-glass-shaded hanging lamp over the table wired for electricity. Another small reading lamp stood on a mellow pecan-wood table by the chair.

On the far wall, away from the center front door, stood the huge brass double bed, covered with a colorful crazy quilt topped by two fluffy goose-down pillows. Crissy had helped her granny make those pillows. Kneeling next to her grandmother, who was seated on a low stool in the shade of the gigantic old oak in back of the house, Crissy had tried to keep the nervous goose lying still on her granny's lap while, with quick, nonhurtful motions, she pulled tiny goose-down fluff from the bird's chest. Never had she slept so well as on that first night using her new pillow. Granny had agreed with her observation, adding sagely, "That's cuz you helped make 'em, honey." And Crissy had learned another lesson about life in the process.

Now, in less than half an hour, Crissy had bathed and was blow-drying her hair into a halo of shiny, dark curls. She was looking forward to her dinner date, and fingered the business card James had given her. A sudden vision of her cute and energetic friend Katie Cohen made her reach quickly for the phone on the nightstand.

Crissy had met her in college, and together they had made quite a team. Now, long after graduation, they remained close friends though separated by hundreds of miles. While Crissy had chosen to come back home to teach, Katie had opted for the big-city life and a lucrative position in an ad agency. In fact, her job had helped to open the corporate doors for Crissy's freelancing on commercials. The phone rang for the fifth time, and Crissy nervously muttered, "Come on! Be at home!" On the sixth ring, Katie answered.

After a short visit, catching up on the latest gossip and possible business opportunities, Katie chirped, "What's up, Crissy? You sound more excited than usual."

"You're right, my friend," Crissy answered. "I met a man this afternoon at work. I'm supposed to have dinner with him later this evening, and it occurred to me that you just might have some info on him. He claims he left New York recently . . . used to work for some big ad agency in town. Now he's here in Branson, starting a toy business, of all things. Says his name is James Robert Prince III. Ever heard of him, honey?"

"You've met the *Prince*?" she squawked in utter disbelief. "You're going to have dinner with him *tonight*? My Lord, Crissy!"

Agitated, Crissy shot back, "Well, what the hell's wrong with him? What do you know? *Tell me!*"

"He's one of the—or rather, I should say, now that he's moved away, he *was*—one of the most eligible bachelors on the East Coast, that's who he is," Katie yelled back. In a quieter tone, but rushing her words, out of excitement, she went on, "For years he's been in every gossip column in town—and always with a different beautiful woman dripping with diamonds or furs, or both, draped on his arm. No one believed him when he said he was leaving the agency—he was the president, Crissy!—and going into another business entirely." She paused for breath. "I just can't believe you met him."

"He stalked me all afternoon while I was doing my routines, and right after the stage show, he cornered me and invited me for the *third time* to have dinner with him," Crissy explained. "He's really a hunk, Katie."

"I'm afraid he could be a hunk of trouble for you, little innocent," Katie grumbled. "Honey, he has a reputation for lovin' and leavin' women. I don't want you to get hurt. He's the original old smoothie, and God knows, he's had enough experience," she muttered, showing her real concern for her friend. "If you do go out with him, you've got to be very, very careful. Do you hear me?"

"I hear you, Katie!" she replied, smiling at the caution in Katie's voice. "I'm really glad I had the inspiration to call you before this date, though. It helps to put everything into perspective. Maybe it's time someone gave *him* a run for his money, huh?"

"Better wear your track shoes, then," Katie shot back. "He's a wolf, Crissy. But, God help me, I'd give two weeks' salary to have a sample of his wares." She chuckled wickedly. "You just be careful, hear?" she ordered, using one of the twangy voices she had learned from Crissy.

"Now, little lamb, don't you fret none," she answered, instantly becoming Tulip, to her friend's accompanying laughter. "Ifen he gits fresh with me, I'll jist have old Pappy come out'en the hills and blow him to smithereens."

"Just don't get caught in the cross fire, Crissy, but have a supergood time tonight, and let me hear how it turns out, okay? I probably won't sleep a wink tonight," she declared stoically. "J. R. Prince III . . . how lucky can you get?"

"The crazy thing is that he was attracted to Tulip. Can you believe that?" she asked. Then she laughed happily, confessing, "I must admit Tulip got carried away with her wanton flirting ways."

"He won't know what to think when you walk into the restaurant tonight, will he? You're going to bowl him over. You're going to be a page out of *Glamour* magazine, I bet."

"Right!" Crissy giggled. "Wish me luck, Katie. I'll talk to you soon." She hung up, then quickly began to dress for her date while making crafty plans to stymie his every overture to romance.

Carefully and professionally she applied her makeup, remembering every trick she had learned in her course in theater cosmetology. Every stroke was understated, but together the final result was pure art. On impulse, she took the time to enamel her long, tapered nails a clear red, to match her lip gloss. She sat back on her vanity bench and surveyed the full effect. She didn't look anything like Tulip Bloom tonight, she decided.

Noting the time, she quickly slipped out of her robe and into white lace bikini panties and hose, and donned her favorite white halter-top, lined sheath dress, every trim inch of her womanly figure enhanced by the quality of the design. She chose extremely high-heeled white strappy sandals so she would feel more confident, being almost eye level with James. She remembered how she'd had to look up at him this afternoon, and then she remembered those cobalt-blue eyes that looked right into her soul. Katie's words of caution echoed in her ears. She knew she had to remember them. Be careful! She was playing with fire tonight, she decided, giggling out loud while she enveloped herself in a cloud of expensive French perfume.

It was seven-thirty when she wrapped the matching fringed shawl around her bare shoulders. The deep triangle completely covered her backless dress. Snatching her small white purse from the golden oak dresser, she hurried out to her car and drove quickly to the Wooden Nickle. She was glad she knew more about him now than when she had first met him. Still, she was having difficulty quieting the butterflies that were flapping around in her chest. After she parked the car, she walked sedately into the lobby and was greeted by the owner, a former high-school friend, Bob Edwards.

"Good evening, Bob," she said, smiling. "Business looks good tonight. I'm glad."

"How are you, little Crissy?" he said with admiration. "You're looking real fine," he complimented her. Before she could tell him she was meeting a friend, he continued, "Your date is already here. I've given him the best table in the house, honey. He's a handsome devil, so I figured he might be someone special to you. Right this way." He led her across the room to the small, intimate table for two. She could feel the eyes of other patrons as they turned to watch her graceful entrance, and she was glad she had taken the time to look her best tonight.

Slowly James rose from his chair. His obvious surprise and disbelief were quickly masked by a more sensuous expression. Bob seated her, and Crissy thanked him in her quiet, well-modulated voice. Then he slipped away without another word. She looked across the table, directly into James's penetrating gaze, and smiled gently. "Good evening, James," she said. "I hope you had no trouble finding this place."

"Good evening, Crissy," he replied in a whisper, his eyes drinking in her beauty as if he would never tire of doing so. He was speechless for a moment. Crissy took the time to admire his handsomely rugged features again and the jacket of his well-cut dark suit. Tonight the stripes in his silk tie matched the dark blue of his eyes. Oh, yes, she thought, this is an attractive man . . . and he knows the power he has! Be careful, country gal, she silently cautioned herself.

Without a word and never taking his dark gaze from her face, he reached across the small table and tenderly lifted her hand to his lips, kissing her fingertips. He sighed, then murmured, "Please excuse my silence just now, Crissy." His eyes continued to burn into hers as he slowly turned her hand in his and branded her palm with a warm, moist kiss that almost caused her to leap to her feet and run for the exit. The heat of his touch was devastating! "I'm overwhelmed. You're absolutely ravishing tonight," he whispered. He kissed her palm again, this time boldly flicking his rough tongue across her skin.

She shivered in spite of her firm control, and gently extricated her hand from his, picking up her menu in an attempt to break the sensuous spell he wove.

"None of my hopes for the future contained any vision as charming and exquisite as you," he murmured. "And in the twinkling of an eye, I find myself frantically rearranging all my dreams."

Surely he couldn't be even remotely serious . . . could he? "Sounds to me as if you could use a good file clerk," she countered lightly. "I know several competent people I could recommend to you."

"I don't want just anybody, Crissy," he replied quietly. "I want you!"

His words hit her like a fist in the stomach. She refused to meet his eyes, because she knew he could set her on fire without so much as lifting a finger. She continued to study the menu and unobtrusively took a deep breath and murmured in a low, noncommittal voice, "I already have a job, James."

For a moment he sat still, but she could feel his eyes burning into her body. Then he picked up his own menu and began to glance over the choices, muttering gruffly, "You'd cost more than I'm prepared to pay anyway!"

Now, what did he mean by that cryptic statement? The safe thing was to change the subject. "The Wooden Nickle is known throughout the area for its excellent steaks. The beef is homegrown, you know," she added, glancing up with an apology when her nerveless foot accidently touched against his leg.

He smiled knowingly. She was embarrassed by their innocent touching, he realized. Perhaps the game wasn't lost yet! "I've been told that the homegrown variety is always the most succulent," he said. "Tender to the lips, sparkling to the taste buds, and appealing to one's appetite." He placed his hand lightly over hers.

He sure wasn't talking about meat on the hoof! Hadn't he claimed it would be open season on two-legged mountain gals by this evening?

Before she could think of a flippant retort, he overrode any objections by adding, "Of course, I believe it's a sign of a sophisticated palate when one has the courage to try the cuisine of other cultures. Sometimes the seasoning is so exotic it burns into one's soul, but then, after the feast, the fiery sensations are quenched in the gentle bouquet of a fine old wine. The adventure of tasting such a rare grape can be repeated, but never exactly duplicated. That's the allure of the unknown. And only the experience can teach us which is worthy of our efforts. Don't you agree?"

Oh, he *was* a sly one! She seethed. She couldn't call him on a thing. He would only deny her objections. I'm just discussing food, Crissy, he would say. Better to ignore the whole disconcerting speech. She met his eyes squarely and requested the small tenderloin with salad and garden peas. Then she drew his attention to the interior design of the restaurant.

"Isn't this place charming?" she asked cheerfully. "All the beams are hand-hewn, and you'll be delighted if you look at the salad bar. It's built around a one-hundred-year-old tree growing right through the roof. Creative, don't you agree?" she added, trying to get him to speak and stop sending those visual messages.

He glanced at the far corner of the room and at her. When he met her gaze again, his eyes were bluer than before, if that was possible. "Very creative," he replied, softly. "I find I'm growing intensely interested in learning more about creative skills. It could be a very educational experience. Could you teach me?"

Well, if he insisted on continuing this farce of a conversation, she'd give him something to chew on for a while. "Mountain folk are suspicious by nature, James," she confided, determined to set him in his place. "Outsiders are always considered suspect. So many have tried to take advantage of us, you see," she went on. "So we don't get involved until they earn our trust. If the newcomer is a flimflam man, he usually hangs *himself* . . . and we don't get hurt."

"I've already told you how much I respect the integrity of the people here. I'm willing to wait. I have the rest of my life to prove I'm sincere," he replied evenly.

She was grateful that the waiter arrived at that

moment, breaking the heavy tension of his words. After James ordered for the two of them, the waiter invited them to try the salad bar. Crissy removed her white fringed shawl, and together they rose from their seats. They stood facing each other, and James caught her hand lightly in his. "You know, it's rather a good thing I was so eager for our evening that I arrived early. You told me you'd be wearing something red . . . that it was your trademark," he said challengingly. "But you didn't, Crissy." His molten gaze wandered to her plunging neckline. "You're dressed all in white."

She laughed musically, sending little ripples of desire coursing through his lean body. "Oh, but I did wear red, James," she contradicted. "You just haven't noticed . . . yet!" Then she turned her back on him, hearing his gasp of surprise, which turned rapidly into a growl of approval.

"That's quite a dress," he muttered, following her as his eyes moved caressingly over her bare, tanned back, dwelling where the fabric hugged the curve of her spine, for there, nestled against her skin, was a large red silk poppy. The air circulating around her graceful erect figure as she walked before him across the room sent the fragile petals fluttering gently in a provocative, come-hither motion.

Crissy was thankful that the mealtime passed pleasantly. James seemed sincere in his effort to get to know her better and to share episodes from his life as well. Either that or he was playing a wait-and-see game.

"Have you always lived here, Crissy?" he asked, pouring more wine into her stemmed glass.

She took an appreciative sip while sorting out just what information she was willing to give him. "No, I went to college in New York City," she told him, smiling at his surprised expression. "Yes, we can discuss some of the landmarks of the Big Apple," she said, answering his unspoken question, "but I seriously doubt we've ever traveled in the same social circles. I went to school on a work-study program and a small scholarship, but I surely had some great experiences while I was there." Then she chuckled, softly. "I doubt old NYC will ever be the same."

"Would you believe I worked my way through college too?" he countered. Her look of disbelief brought a small smile to his lips, contradicted by his gorgeous deep dimples.

Wow! What a smile, Crissy thought. It's just like that country song says—I could be thrown into jail for what I'm thinking right now. But she judiciously kept her thoughts to herself and just shook her head at his question, while her flesh quivered.

"Well, I did!" he continued. "Luckily, I had all this excess energy, so I could work three part-time jobs to get my degree in business management. What did you study?" he asked, aware of her concerted examination of his smile. He thought he might tease her about it, but decided against it. She was far too intelligent . . . and refreshingly innocent, he guessed perceptively.

"I studied theater and speech," she answered, lifting her eyes to his, feeling a new respect for his dedication to succeed.

"With your acting ability, I can't understand why you didn't stay in New York and take Broadway by storm," he replied, visibly puzzled. "You'd be a star by now."

She studied her glass, rubbing her fingertip around the rim, before she answered. "I wanted to teach more than act. Besides, I still get to act." A serene smile lifted her red, full lips. "Tulip is one of my favorite characters."

He brought her hand to his warm mouth again, this time kissing each fingertip in sensual delight. "But who are you, Crissy Brant?" he asked in a whisper, his eyes shining with curiosity. "You have the vitality and humor of Tulip, yet tonight, you've remained aloof, calm, and cool, but I can feel your hidden passion even in your delicate hands. I want to know you better. You've bewitched me, sweetheart. When are you acting?

Or could you be the answer to this man's dream of one woman's ability to be everything he ever hoped for? Tell me, Crissy. Who are you?"

Drawing deeply on her training to conceal her churning emotions, she extricated her fingers from his control and smiled mysteriously into his serious blue eyes. "That will have to remain my secret, James."

"And 'trust' is the key word, right?" A string of swear words boomeranged around in his brain. How in the world was he ever going to tear down her wall of suspicions?

She only smiled again and lowered her eyes to her wineglass, carefully studying the changing patterns reflected by the candlelight. She could feel he was withdrawing from his attack on her emotions. Good! She had won this small scrimmage, but she wondered if she could hope to win the war.

He took up the reins of conversation, telling her about his new home, almost completed on the lake. His voice carried his enthusiasm as he discussed the energy-saving features he was incorporating into the design. It included passive solar technology, which interested Crissy too. The rest of their meal was punctuated by eager nods of agreement and smiling understanding as they found the safe conversational middle ground of common interest. Eventually, as the restaurant began to clear, he murmured, "I'd like to show you my new home, Crissy. Let me take you there tomorrow."

"I have to work tomorrow," she reminded him. "Perhaps another day."

"What are you afraid of, Crissy?" There was cold steel in his low voice. "I'm not going to eat you alive, you know."

She trembled inwardly, but laughed lightly, at his words. "Gracious, I should hope not! You've just eaten enough to last for days. Will you excuse me for a moment?" she asked, pleasantly surprised when James also rose graciously. She smiled seductively then, giving him just a little food for thought. When she turned to go to the powder room, he seated himself again and sipped his wine, watching her as she moved—she could feel his eyes burning into her skin.

She couldn't begin to understand the impact his attention had upon her senses, and she wasn't going to try. Not now! What she needed to do was to put some mileage between them. Quickly she bypassed the ladies' room and scooted out the kitchen door, waving to the chef and his assistants—all good friends—and urgently hissed, "You don't know me! *You never saw me!*"

They waved in return, nodding in understanding. She breathed deeply of the cool night air, pulling her shawl tightly around her bare shoulders. She was glad she had thought to complain a little about the indoor temperature before she left the table. Walking stealthily around the building, she quickly unlocked her car and drove away quietly even though every cell in her tense body screamed that she should make a fast exit.

Within twenty minutes she had arrived at her little cabin, well off the beaten path of tourists' haunts and almost impossible to find unless one knew it was there. Yet she could still feel the heat of James's eyes boring into her, and she furtively pulled the car around to the back.

And when she got inside, she moved by moonlight streaming through her windows, not choosing to turn on any lights, unwilling to ask herself why. After she undressed, she opened the window by her big brass bed, letting in the cool breezes and the night sounds of woodland insects and small creatures. She lay down, feeling the smooth sheets on her nude body. Usually the silky texture of the covers soothed her skin, but tonight she felt as if she could burst into flames. How could one man cause so much disruption in such a short time? Seeking the escape of sleep, she decided she would not see James again. But the mist of unconsciousness was a long time coming.

Three

Late the following morning, Crissy was entertaining a rapt gathering of tourists as they stood beneath one of the many shade trees that were scattered along the winding streets of the little made-for-amusement town. Silver Dollar City had become, over the years, through wise and well-planned advertising and promotion, a national attraction for summertime fun. It was a gathering place for a variety of gifted craftspeople and artists. The maze of serpentine pathways and narrow streets, following the natural contours of the gently rolling hills, led the visitors to dozens of weather-worn, turn-of-the-century frontier shops, where "country folk" dressed in homespun costumes, exhibited their wares and demonstrated their skills.

When these skills had actually been practiced, most had been for survival, while a few, like the making of homemade taffy and peanut-brittle candy, were purely for tasty pleasure. Gunsmiths and pewter-dish makers showed how to work with metals; an elderly, bewhiskered man made brooms from hand-carved tree limbs and dried prairie grasses; wood-carvers, standing ankle-deep in curled wood shavings, uncovered, with their sharp tools, the wood nymphs in driftwood and a six-foot regal Indian chief out of a hefty, air-dried walnut log. Quilter and corn-husk-doll maker, weaver and puffing glassblower, soap maker and tintype photographer—these were among the fascinating collection of people who knew the old ways and were intent on passing along to today's generation the heritage of our emerging nation.

In her own way, Crissy, using the character of Tulip, was able to impart the folklore and legends of her beloved Ozark Mountains. She took pride in that fact; not everyone had the ability to mesmerize the vacationers with the yarns and nonsense of the hills, entertaining people while educating them about a different culture.

At the moment, she was embarking on another long-winded story about a "revenooer" that she had decided to tell when she found out that one member of her audience was on vacation from his job in an Arkansas whiskey distillery. It seemed this particularly hapless "revenooer" was determined to catch her Grandpappy Bloom whilst he was tendin' his still, deep in a secret clearing, hidden in the forest.

"Grandpappy warn't no fool," she told the group conspiratorially. "He knowed that revenooer were hot on his trail. Shucks," she said, slapping her hand against her thigh, "he done laid a track a mile wide jist so's he could trap 'em." She chuckled. "Well, that danged fool walked, big as you please, right smack dab inter the middle of that clearin', and Grandpappy called the watch-boars on 'em . . ." She stopped then, her timing flawless, as several in the group raised quizzical eyebrows while a brave few asked in disbelief, "Watch-*boars*?"

She sidled over to the man from Arkansas and held him with her steady gaze. "Shucks, mister, do yo'all think razorbacks only live in Ar-kan-saw?" Then she continued her story, describing in detail how the scared man ran when her Grandpappy set the wild boars a-snappin' at his britches. She became the snorting, dangerous wild pigs in her story, gnashing her teeth and making excited, horrific grunting noises, changing in a twinkling to the huffing, puffing "revenooer," running for his life. "And that's the last time Grandpappy were ever bothered by *that* lawman," she ended, smiling happily when the group burst into appreciative applause.

A little blonde girl pulled shyly at Crissy's skirt and asked, "Why is your name Tulip?" Her green eyes danced, showing the obvious picture she had conjured in her mind.

Crissy returned her smile and was preparing to begin her charming, imaginative tale about Tulip Bloom, when she felt two strong hands fasten on her shoulders in an iron grasp. She glanced up quickly and met a pair of fiery blue eyes that held a threat in their snapping anger. She gasped aloud, then looked him over. His lean body was covered by a pair of tight, well-worn jeans and a muted plaid western shirt under a soft leather vest. A Stetson hat was on his head at a jaunty angle. He looked like the Marlboro Man!

"Smile!" James commanded beneath his breath, his wide grin an artificial slash across his stern features. At once she did as he ordered, knowing he meant business.

"Folks," he said, using his best down-home drawl. "I hope you'll forgive me for stealin' little Tulip from you for a while," he declared, widening his smile as his eyes swiftly captured the group. "You see, it's time for our break now . . . and I don't get her alone *nearly* enuf." He chuckled, winking knowingly at one of the men. "I'm sure you understand," he ended wickedly. Then he looked down at Crissy as if she were the most important thing in his life, and crooned, "Say goodbye, Tulip, darlin'."

Quickly he led her away from the gawking, tittering tourists, pulling her to his side, effectively cutting off any hope she might have had to escape. In seconds he walked her into a small grove of trees, spinning her around by her shoulders and catching her arms against her sides. When she tried to step away from him, she backed right into a tree, which seemed to be exactly where James wanted her. Trapped!

He was angry, and of course Crissy didn't need a crystal ball to figure out the reason, but she refused to speak first. Finally he broke the icy silence. "Why did you walk out on me last night, Ms. Brant?"

Searching frantically for a way to humor him, she became Tulip, and drawled, with a nervous grin upon her trembling lips, "I was kidnapped by a band of crazed mountain men?"

His scowl told her she had missed the mark. She tried again. "I remembered an urgent appointment."

"Dammit, Crissy, stop playing games and stop running. I want to know why you felt it was so damned necessary to leave without telling me. I acted like a damned fool when no one would tell me where you lived," he barked. "I think those people in the kitchen suspected that I was some kind of a sex maniac." His frown grew harsh as he recalled with chagrin his ranting and raving when the kitchen help kept telling him they didn't know a Crissy and had never seen her before, even when he described her in detail.

She couldn't suppress a smile at his frustrating experience, promising herself that she'd make it up to her friends for their protection last night. "I told you we give outsiders enough rope to hang themselves," she needled softly, feeling safer now that some of his anger had dissipated.

"Especially outsiders who move too fast, right?" Her nod of agreement only added to his self-chastisement. "I don't have any ready excuse, Crissy. I think I just got carried away with your beauty last night," he told her contritely. "My mind keeps telling me to keep my nose to the grindstone—business as usual—but the rest of me is saying that you're a very special person . . . and I shouldn't let you out of my sight for a minute." He appeared somewhat embarrassed that he'd put these thoughts into words. "I want to know you better. So much better." He sighed, releasing her arms from his hold, and took a step backwards.

"I know I must have frightened you away last night, Crissy," he said, taking a deep breath to control himself. "Won't you please accept my apology for acting like an idiot, so we can begin all over again?" He met her suspicious gaze and swallowed nervously to remove the lump of pride in his throat. *"Please?"*

She could hardly believe her ears; his voice held so much sincerity. Was it possible he realized his mistake and really wanted to begin again? "That was quite a humble speech for a city feller," she drawled, becoming Tulip again because her own heart was beating double-time with her renewed interest in him.

"Crissy, don't hide." He groaned. "Talk to me, honey," he begged.

The poor man really looked as if he had lost his last friend, Crissy thought sympathetically. "It's just that I'm having a very difficult time being myself right now," she explained in her own voice, wavering though it was. "I'll admit I had every intention of knocking you down a peg or two last night." A swift jolt of regret cut into her heart when he nodded, acknowledging that she had succeeded. "But in a very short time, I realized I was over my head in our little game of matching wits. James, you're a pro at keeping a girl off balance . . . and I just couldn't cope," she confessed with embarrassment.

He grasped her hands against his broad chest, looking like a little boy who had just gotten his heart's desire on Christmas morning. His eyes shone with an innocence she had not seen during their short time together. "Do you mean we can begin all over again, Crissy?" he asked in suppressed excitement. "You're going to give me another chance?"

Her heart melted when she looked into his eyes, warm with hope and good intentions. "Yes," she answered quietly. "It means we can begin all over again."

"Let's seal the bargain with a kiss," he murmured, bringing her pliant body against his length. He was going to kiss her, she knew that. But she continued to look deeply into his wonder-filled eyes and watched, like a rabbit caught in a snare. The innocence faded, replaced by the fiery heat of triumph.

That wily fox! she thought in momentary surprise. He's a better actor than I am. He should get an Oscar for this performance . . . and he's getting his own way . . . again! Just before his lips covered hers, she mentally shrugged. She wanted to kiss him, and surrendered to her emotions.

But his warm, sensuous lips never completed their journey to her parted, inviting mouth. The clanging announcement of her next show made them jump apart like two kids caught behind the barn. "I've got a show to do," she exclaimed, still breathless from the near kiss.

As she turned to run to the stage, James caught hold of her wrist and pulled her hard against him. "We'll continue this discussion after work, okay?" he asked in silken tones, sure of his appeal to her now. She nodded dumbly, pushed away from his circle of attraction, and hurried to the outdoor stage, where her partners waited for her arrival.

The show's opening was always the same, but the three had found through experience that many of the stories and jokes had to be tailored for each audience. Sometimes the people could be led through the show like carefree, enthusiastic children; on other days they were what was called, in show-business jargon, a "tough crowd." Today seemed one of those days.

As the show progressed, Crissy decided to go out into the group and work her magic at close range. The members of the audience clapped their approval of her arrival in their midst. She glanced to the right and spotted James sitting on the same bench he had occupied the day before. She sauntered over and let loose with a mountain yell that, had it been any higher-pitched, would have shattered a few eardrums, but the crowd was with her now.

She stood before James and wiggled her hips while she puffed up her oversized sleeves and polished the tips of her beat-up boots on the backs of her legs, smiling devilishly all the while. He sat perfectly still, but his bright gaze told her he was looking forward to whatever she was going to do next.

"Well, land's sake," she exclaimed, "woodja lookie here, folks. Here sits my favor-rite couzin, come home fer a visit." She jumped into his lap, bringing an explosive "oofff!" from James. His arms instantly snaked around her waist, and Crissy trembled slightly, despite herself, at his touch. She kept right on smiling into his handsome face, but her eyes began to sparkle with the excitement of her plans for him. And he wouldn't be able to do a thing about it, not in this crowd! She was determined to make him pay for his playacting, which had melted her heart and convinced her of his good intentions a while ago in the little grove nearby.

"This here is Jimmy Bob. He's part of the Bloom clan, but we ain't seed him fer years 'n years," she continued, brazenly running her fingertips along his eyebrows and down his cheeks, dwelling for a moment to trace his pliant mouth and tickle his moustache. When he bared his straight white teeth, intending to nip at her hand, she quickly pinched his cheek and playfully pulled his ear. "Youse all growed up now, ain't you?" She batted her thick lashes. "Youse a *man*!" she crooned, running her hands through his hair. When his hold on her tightened, she only chuckled deep in her throat, and he pulled her even closer.

One of her partners on the stage called to her, "Ere he be our kissin' couzin, little gal?"

She hungrily gazed into James's face and stage-whispered, "He *surely* be, Jesse."

"Then, you oughter say howdy with a good ole

Ozark Mountain greetin', sister," he hollered. "But do he remember what that be?"

"Does you?" she asked innocently.

James solemnly shook his head. "I can't say I remember. Suppose you tell me what it is, Tulip Bloom."

Thinking to herself that James made a wonderful straight man, she silently wound her arms around his neck and buried her fingers in his thick, wavy locks, cuddling ever closer in his arms. "A Ozark Mountain greetin' is when Tulip-s-s-s presses on yours," she explained wickedly, then kissed him full on the mouth.

She was not prepared for his response, which threatened to take her breath away. He lifted his hands from her waist and ran them along her ribs to press her hard against him. His thumbs, though still, burned through the thin fabric of her "Daisy Mae" blouse and brought a throbbing awareness of his touch to her breasts. Suddenly, she was crushed to his chest. The warmth of his ragged breath washed over her flushed cheeks and gave evidence of his eager participation. What had first begun as a light, whimsical smooch grew into a deepening kiss that demanded her response.

For a moment she was lost to her emotions, caring little that the people around her were beginning to roar in good-natured humor. Finally she came back to her senses, and pulled away, croaking. "Whoa! Jimmy Bob. Yore city-slicker ways is fixin' to overcharge my batter-ees!"

And although he released her, she heard his satisfied sigh and his gasping retort. "So *that*'s where you got your name. Your two lips would make any man bloom!" He chuckled at her scowling expression when she realized he had also repaid her for making fun of *his* name yesterday. Outwitted again, she thought fuming. In seconds she had scampered back on stage, and together, she and her partners wound up the show to a rousing conclusion and were rewarded with thunderous applause from their happy audience.

As the crowd left, James continued to sit on the

bench, watching Crissy reset her props. He was in a bemused state of mind. What a woman, he thought in delight. One thing was sure: He would never know what she might think of next. He chuckled happily. And what a kiss! If she hadn't been playing Tulip, she would have slapped his face, he decided. He got up then, knowing he'd better walk. He was getting carried away with his own fantasies.

Throughout Crissy's workday, James was her shadow, staying at the outer edge of any circle of tourists listening to her homespun tales of adventure in the hills. When she had a break, he was waiting to stroll at her side as they wandered along the winding streets of the little town. They watched the wood carvers, Crissy's favorite among all the crafts people and artists, as one fashioned a weathered-creased old boot from a bit of pine and another demonstrated the advanced skills of his profession as he created a mountain scene in relief, carving on a solid oak door a little log cabin nestled among the tall pines. A rushing brook and waterfall cut down the tall mountain in the background. Above the carving, an oval window of art glass had been inserted. The only color in the leaded clear glass was the profile of a bright red cardinal perched upon a dark brown limb, at the end of which sprouted three springtime-green leaves. It was a beautiful composition, and James and Crissy spent several minutes just admiring it and four other finished products, each containing a different scene and window design.

"I like the redbird best of all, don't you?" she asked James. "He looks so real, sitting there all proud and puffed up. I'm just waiting for him to start singing." She laughed musically when James began to whistle a playful rendition of the bird's mating call. He took her hand and they began to walk again, stopping next to listen as the soap-making lady told how she used lard and lye to make her product.

"Hey, Tulip, gal," the older woman teased. "If this

be the new feller you been sparkin', best you git some of my soap so's you kin be ready to do his shirts."

Crissy played right along with her chuckling sister-employee, Sarah. "Shucks, Granny," Tulip replied scornfully. "I's a lib-er-a-ted woman. If'n this here feller is hankerin' to wed with me, he's gonna hafta scrub his own shirts!"

James put his arm around her shoulders and whispered into her ear in a sensual growl, "I won't mind scrubbing my shirts, if you'll scrub my back!" She twisted from his hold and gasped in astonishment when she caught the dancing light in his clear blue eyes. Then, face flaming, she mumbled good-bye to the woman and swiftly walked away, feeling totally alarmed at James's one-upmanship, when she heard his hearty laughter and call to wait up for him.

Later they both looked as if they had been caught in a quirkish summer snowfall after feasting on warm, deep-fried funnel cake, an old-time dessert made from sweetened pancake batter measured into a large kitchen funnel into which the cook stuck her fingertip to hold the thick mixture. Then she would release the pointed spout, letting the dough flow out the tube into the bubbling-hot oil, making swirling patterns the size of a platter. Within moments, the dough browned on one side like a French pastry and was turned over. The cook drained it and placed the sizzling-hot delicacy on a paper plate and sprinkled it liberally with powdered sugar. And although most of the sweet confection stuck to the dessert, a goodly amount was distributed over the willing diner as he or she ate. Even the breath from one's nose blew the weightless white around with each bite.

Laughing, they spent an additional five minutes brushing away the incriminating evidence of their splendid treat, agreeing that the tasty funnel cake was worth the added clean-up effort. James seemed particularly delighted to find some elusive sugar on the red tulip perched atop Crissy's whimsical straw hat. When he offered to kiss the stickiness from her lips, she pouted prettily and shook her head, leading him to the water fountain, where they wet their napkins and finished the job properly.

When Crissy got back home after work and was preparing for another date with James, she was struck by one thought: They had enjoyed each other's company today! James really seemed like a very fine man. A little forceful at times, but nice just the same.

He had insisted on picking her up for their date this evening, but Crissy had been equally adamant in her refusal. "I'll meet you there," she said, ignoring his frown of disapproval, and smiling charmingly at his little-boy pout at not getting his way when he accused her of bringing along her personal get-away car. But when she challenged him with the question, "Will I need to escape from you again tonight?" he was quick to reassure her that he would be on his best behavior, promising he would be a perfect gentleman. He would do nothing to jeopardize the time they spent together, he vowed.

Crissy sighed contentedly as she slipped behind the wheel of her car and reached for the ignition key. This evening they would meet at the Rustic Oak, another fine restaurant in the area.

When she arrived, James was waiting for her. He had chosen to stay outside this time, he told her, so they could enter together. "At least now I know what kind of car you drive. I should have known it would be red! Besides, it's such a warm, beautiful evening," he added, his eyes lingering on her light gray halter-top dress, which revealed her tanned smooth shoulders and back and the area between her firm breasts in the deep V neckline. His eyebrow lifted in a silent salute when he noticed, almost as an afterthought, the vivid red silk kerchief knotted around her slender neck, its perky tips at a jaunty angle to her chin.

His eyes were sending Crissy those messages again, and she was appalled at the graphic mental pictures that were flooding her mind. To break the spell, she flicked her fingertips at the little scarf and proclaimed in a light voice, "My trademark, you know."

But she was completely disconcerted when she heard his quick response. "For passion, no doubt."

"Or rage," she shot back, striding away.

He lengthened his step, easily catching her at the door. Lifting her hand to his lips, he caught her fiery gaze with eyes that were deep with hidden meaning. "No fighting tonight, Crissy. I was only teasing, honey. Forgive me?"

Now, Crissy knew intellectually that he was putting on his good-little-boy act again, but nevertheless, she felt her heart melt under his steady scrutiny. She sighed in surrender and smiled tremulously as he led her into the cozy restaurant and requested a secluded table for two.

They both ordered fresh lake trout, and she knew, no matter what they had decided upon, that the food would be done to perfection, because here again she was among her friends, who would bend over backwards to give her and James their best service and their best cooking. James remarked about the attentive service and Crissy agreed, sending a secretive wink of thanks to their smiling waiter, Bill Manchester, another high-school friend.

James kept his word, making light conversation and laughing when she caught his subtle humor with a witty response of her own. He delighted in their companionable conversation, wondering if they would mesh together on *all* levels . . . hoping that they would. "Are you enjoying yourself, Crissy?" he asked after they had been trading childhood tales of adventure.

She nodded, tracing her slim fingertip along the stem of her wineglass. "I had no idea how hard you'd worked to get where you are today, James. I'm truly impressed," she murmured. He'd disclosed that he had come from a very poor family in Brooklyn and had been working since he was nine years old, when he began earning his own way by doing odd jobs.

"Are your parents still living?" she asked cautiously, hoping at least one of them still had parents. Hers had been gone for a long time now.

The look of pain that crossed his face told her the answer before he spoke. "That's one of the things I wish I could change," he replied sadly. "I could do so much for them now . . . but they died before I had the chance. I loved them very much, Crissy. Neither one of them ever had any doubt that I would be successful. It's the one thing that kept me going sometimes," he added, his eyes revealing the hard times he had seen before he had gotten to the top.

"And I'm sure they loved you very much," she said, unable to stop herself from reaching across the table and covering his tense hand with hers. "The fact that you've overcome so many obstacles and have your own business now would be reward enough for their faith in you. I feel very sure that would be the case, James. My parents gave me that same sort of blind support."

"Your parents are gone too?" he asked. Again she nodded, feeling words were unnecessary. "I have a sister—she's younger than I am," he said. "She's the one with all the brains. Julie has her Ph.D. in virology. She works in New York at one of the foremost oncology research facilities in the world," he added with evident pride.

"Cancer research," exclaimed Crissy with respect. "Is she trying to prove some forms of that terrible disease are caused by virus?"

"That's exactly what she's trying to prove," James said, struck once again by Crissy's intelligence. "She's so dedicated to her goal that poor Tom Sinclair, her fiancé, has one devil of a time getting her to come out of her lab long enough to plan their wedding." He chuckled, unaware of the shocked expression that crossed Crissy's features and disappeared almost at once. "I'm surprised he got her to stand still long enough to accept his proposal!"

"Is he in research too?" she asked, longing to hear that he was also a doctor.

He laughed outright now. "I suppose you could say he's in research of a sort, but actually he's one of the lead admen in my former company, J-R Advertising Agency," he explained. "I was the person who introduced them, and Cupid caught them with their defenses down." He grinned at Crissy. "Tom was working on a big ad campaign for a major pharmaceutical company and he needed information so he could understand some of their more complicated processes. I knew Julie could help him out, so I invited them both to dinner one night . . . and that's all she wrote!" he informed her. "It was love at first fight! Of course, they claim they just take part in heated intellectual discussions, and who am I to doubt their word? Anyway, it's quite obvious they love each other, and if they can swing it, they'll be married at Thanksgiving."

Crissy was worried. Tom Sinclair was a friend. He had worked for her contract employer, International Advertising, before he had moved on to a more lucrative position. He had dated her close friend Katie for a while, two years ago. She made a mental note to call him as soon as she got home tonight—no matter what the hour and that she might wake him up. She had to get his promise of secrecy should they ever meet in James's presence. That was an unlikely possibility, but still she had to cover herself for any contingency. She didn't trust James Prince as far as she could throw his big, beautiful body! Not yet, anyway. She was still a mountain gal who looked with a skeptical eye upon newcomers.

Her troubling train of thought was broken when James asked if she had any brothers or sisters. "I'm not alone, if that's what you mean," she answered jauntily, determined not to give him the information that she had been alone for years. Then she began to tell him about her "fantasy family," which, over the years, after hours of tale-telling and playacting, seemed almost real to her. She had the story down pat because she used it often to scare away unwanted suitors or men who wanted a one-night stand. "I have an older brother. Johnny is thirty-two, and about twice as big as you! He's on the road a lot of the time in his sales job," she told him, putting on her best smile of love and affection. "His wife, Billy, and their baby girl, Crissy, Junior, stay with me sometimes," she added for good measure, so he wouldn't assume she lived alone.

"What's your real name, Crissy?"

"Wild horses couldn't drag that information from me," she replied with fire in her eyes. He just shook his head and chuckled, wondering if a man could be married for fifty years and still not know his wife's full name. "Then, I have my Granny Brant," she continued, smiling again when she described her real granny, who had died when Crissy was a teenager. "She's one of the original mountain women, you know," she said, warming to her subject when James leaned forward to hear about her legendary grandmother. "She chews tobaccee and kin still handle her 12-gauge right handy!" she said in Tulip's voice. "Yes, siree, now, *that*'s a true mountain gal. She kin hit a gopher right between the eyes at twenty yards."

"I'd like to meet her sometime," James said enthusiastically. Or was he trying to prove that Granny didn't exist?

"She doesn't like townfolk, as a rule," Crissy hastened to explain. "Most of the time I have to go up into the hills to visit her, but sometimes I can coax her home for a short visit. About every three months I get my way." She laughed. "After all, she's the one who made me so independent and stubborn. In many ways she's been like a mother to me. You see, my mom died when I was a little girl, and Granny raised me, mostly . . . when she could catch me, that is!" She was feeling a little guilty at her blatant tale-telling and wanted to get off the subject. "I wouldn't want you to meet her," she told James. "You'd only get into an argument about why she let me grow up so contrary."

But he wasn't put off by her flippancy. "No," he replied. "I'd like to thank her for doing such a wonderful job with you. Not only are you a beautiful, intelligent woman, but you give pleasure and joy to those around you," he added with all seriousness.

"Ah, shucks, Mr. Prince. Ifen yo'all don't stop, I'll git sich a swelled hade!" she exclaimed, blushing pink and rosy.

"You're hiding again," he reminded her, but he leaned back into a relaxed position in his comfortable chair, showing with his body that he was taking a step away from her so she wouldn't feel threatened. Yes, he thought, she might be a grown woman, but she had such an air of innocence about her. He'd like to take care of her. She sure could use it, too, but she was so damned independent!

They finished their meal and were enjoying an after-dinner brandy; the room was filled with the melody of a love song. "Do you like to dance?" Crissy asked forthrightly.

He leaned forward again and took her hand in his. "I'd like to dance with *you*," he answered without hesitation. "Can you arrange it, honey?" he asked, his eyes beginning to send heated messages of his desire to hold her in his arms. "Is that a live band I hear?"

"It's live, all right, and the dance floor is downstairs, in the lounge," she replied. "Shall we?"

Within a short time, James had paid the tab and left several folded bills on the table for their waiter's excellent service. And with Crissy leading the way, he escorted her down the wide, carpeted staircase to the lounge area, which was dimly lit and filled with atmosphere.

"Mmmmm," he whispered, his arm moving firmly around her slim waist. "I think I'm gonna *love* this place!"

They were seated in a corner booth, its deep curve allowing them to sit side by side, with the table in front. After they ordered gin and tonics, he turned to her and gently kissed her flushed cheek. Crissy reminded herself that she would have to nurse this new drink for the rest of the evening or she wouldn't have the power of mind to outmaneuver James's amorous moves. Yet she nodded in agreement when he murmured, "Shall we?" and led her to the small dance floor. She *wanted* to dance with him . . . to be held in his arms.

It seemed to Crissy that they had always danced together. His skill during this slow dance was both confident and sensual. He drew her firmly against his rhythmic length, clasping her hand between them so that her palm could feel the heat of his body through his soft silk shirt while his knuckles brushed innocently over the upper swell of her right breast. Surely, she thought breathlessly, he can feel my heart beating as if I've just run two miles! If he did, he gave no indication. Unless one could count the way his left hand slid around her bare back, down along her spine, to settle at the lower curve of her waist. "You're a very good dancer, James," she complimented, feeling her full skirt sweep against her legs.

His only response was to pull her closer and whisper in her ear. "This is where you belong, sweetheart. Right here in my arms. You fit just right." He kissed her earlobe and circled the edge with his tongue. She shivered against him, certain now that he knew her reaction to his touch. She closed her eyes and surrendered to the heavenly hold of his arms around her soft, swaying form.

They danced through three love songs, which made up a set. Crissy could feel the silken web of his sensual trap spinning tighter and tighter around her throbbing heart. It was with a sense of relief, then, that she heard the band begin to play a disco tune, which heralded a less intimate style of dancing . . . or so Crissy thought. She looked up into James's handsome face, giggled, and became Tulip. "Hey, city feller, kin you do this here newfangled stuff?" she asked, fully expecting he would defer to the younger crowd and take her back to their booth.

His clear blue eyes grew smoky and warm at the same moment. His body began to gyrate in a very provocative manner, and he reached down to unbutton the expensive jacket of his gray suit. "Can I do this stuff? Honey, I was a gold-card member of Studio 54 in its heyday," he informed her drolly. Then he grinned his challenge, his thick moustache curving wickedly. "The question is . . . can a mountain gal keep up with me?"

Her look of disbelief quickly faded, to be replaced by her own determination to accept his challenge. "Well, let's get down!" she growled, perfectly following his intricate steps to the throbbing beat of the music.

"Allll right!" he cheered, rubbing his hands together and praising her magnificent body with his flashing blue eyes. Soon it didn't matter if there were other couples on the floor—James and Crissy had eyes only for each other. Their dancing was a not so subtle fertility ritual. Their thrusting hips and swaying shoulders moved up against the other's, then pulled away in erotic movements. His gaze dropped to her provocative breasts, quivering against her halter top, and flames of pleasure lit his eyes. She forgot where she was as James moved around her, using his outstretched arms to continually force her closer and closer to his pulsating torso. Finally he made a loose circle around her body, not actually touching her, as she twisted within her limited boundaries, pressing one leg, then the other, along his tightly muscled thigh in a wild, uninhibited dance of desire. When the music ended, they clung to each other in breathless abandon and silently walked back to their table.

After they had caught their breaths and drunk deeply, he put his arm around her shoulders and confidently unknotted her red silk kerchief. He slipped it away from her warm skin and leaned over to place a shattering kiss against the sensitized cord. "I was right all along, baby," he crooned, continuing his erotic, pleasure-giving journey along her trembling bare shoulder. He chuckled deep in his chest and reversed his course, back to the throbbing pulse-point in her throat. "It's a wonder the management didn't call the fire department to put out the blaze," he teased softly.

Crissy was suddenly aware of the exhibition she must have made of herself and she was embarrassed beyond words. She tried gently to retrieve her scarf from his entwined fingers, but he refused to let go. "Let me keep this as a remembrance of our evening, Crissy. I'll replace it, I promise," he said convincingly. She shrugged her shoulders as if it didn't mean that much to her anyway, and sipped her drink to fill the silence.

She was relieved at first when a long-stemmed young woman, dressed in tight satin trousers and a silver lamé bandeau top, sauntered up to their table. She looked as if she were enjoying her first summer of legal drinking. She gazed fetchingly into James's upturned features, and Crissy felt a stab of pain somewhere around the area of her heart when she saw him quickly peruse the bold woman's curvaceous shape with a measuring eye.

"Hi, I'm Betty Jo," she greeted him, completely ignoring the sudden challenge in Crissy's glare. "Wanna get down?" she asked in a low drawl. "You move better than any man *I've* ever known." She ran her long, polished nails along his jacket sleeve while giving him her best come-hither look.

James smiled warmly at the young woman's words of praise, but he shook his head in refusal. "It's nice to meet you, Betty Jo, but I'm afraid I can't dance with you." He glanced over at Crissy, who now had her emotions well under control and was sitting sedately at his side, wondering what he was going to use as an excuse. "You see, I'm taken. I don't think my fiancée would approve." When he felt Crissy getting ready to explode at his words, he gracefully rose and brought her along with him. "And we were just about to leave when you came over. Thank you for asking," he added, giving the young woman another warm smile and leading Crissy to the stairs.

"Why didn't you just tell the poor girl the truth?" she grated out between clenched teeth. "That you were too tired to dance anymore." She knew she was insulting him, but she didn't care. She was fed up with his overbearing ways. Had she been honest with herself, she would have admitted she was jealous and trying to get back at him.

"But I'm not tired, honey," he contradicted smoothly. "I was ready to leave and I wanted to let Betty Jo down easy." He smiled when Crissy gasped at his conceit.

"You lied!" she challenged. "I'm not your fiancée."

"Not yet, you aren't," was all he tossed back. As she walked from the restaurant and breathed the cool, clear air, she tried to rid herself of the black cloud of anger that swirled around her tousled curly head. She balked when he led her to his low-slung silver sports car and opened the door.

"I'm not going anywhere in your car," she told him firmly. "I'm going home."

"Not yet, you aren't," he repeated, guiding her forcefully into the passenger seat. "We're going someplace to talk."

A dual shiver of fear and longing coursed through her slim body. She knew she should have fought her way out of the car, but the dark side of her soul called to her. He's not going to hurt you, it said. He isn't a thing like that bastard who had hurt her in the past. You can give him the benefit of the doubt, at least. And that was the decision she had reached by the time James slid into the driver's seat. But she was damned if she was going to let him know it!

"Just where do you think you're taking me, Mr.

Prince?" she asked in scathing tones. "I want you to know I'm coming with you under duress."

"Your objection will be duly noted in the minutes," he replied in his best business voice. "But we're going to talk . . . and I think I know the ideal place. We're going to the lake."

In the dark interior of the car, Crissy smiled knowingly, guessing he was going to the best parking spot in the area. Talk, he says. Ha! And at his age! And she forced herself to sit rigidly at his side, her eyes turned to the side window as if she were angry and bored at the same time. Inside, her stomach was doing flip-flops. She couldn't remember the last time she'd gone down to the lake to park. And she'd never gone there with a grown *man*!

A nearly full moon was playing along the surface of the still water when James pulled into a spot beneath the trees bordering the lake. He pressed a button on his door, and all the windows rolled down to let the warm breeze waft in. He sighed in disgust, and Crissy could not help asking, "What's the matter?" But his only answer was a real groan of pain when he wondered aloud what had ever possessed him to buy a little sports car with bucket seats and a five-on-the-floor gearbox between them.

She tried to suppress her laughter, but it was inevitable that she should chuckle at his obvious displeasure at not being able to get close to her. Therefore she was not surprised when he unfolded himself from behind the steering wheel and came around to open the door for her, grasping her hand to assist her, as he said, "We'll walk for a while. All right?"

Crissy agreed, and they walked beneath the bower of tree branches, arm in arm. Just when she felt her nerves settling and her breathing coming under her own control again, he turned her against him and kissed her with such erotic passion that she pushed away from him in fear and confusion. That kiss had definitely been executed by a man . . . not some young fellow just trying his wings. James knew what he was doing. And it scared the hell out of Crissy.

He refused to release her twisting body from his embrace, but immediately began to kiss her slowly, deeply, and thoroughly as he willed her to relax in his arms and return his kiss.

Her body took over from her clamoring brain and did exactly as James wished. Her head fell back against his encircling arm, and he took advantage of her in this unguarded moment to begin the sensuous blazing trail of dangerous kisses to the warm valley between her throbbing breasts. His other hand dropped to her waist and arched her trembling body into his hips, making her fully aware of his arousal. Continuing to kiss her skin, he moved his mouth over the gentle swell of her breasts, murmuring brokenly, "Love me, Crissy. Kiss me. Don't hide from me, honey."

She felt her hands move to his shoulders, and, of their own will, her fingers were buried in the thick, wavy hair at his nape. He raised his head to her throat, then her cheek, and finally fastened warmly and possessively upon her parted, inviting mouth, drinking deeply of the intimate sweetness as his thrusting tongue dueled with hers. She melted into his body, unable to fight anymore. His power to overcome her reluctance was astounding. She had never had any trouble keeping other men in their place when their intentions ran along the same lines. Why was it different with him? Suddenly she knew. She was falling in love with this man of steel . . . and she didn't *want* to stop!

Somehow her change of heart must have been telegraphed to James, because his kiss deepened steadily and he moaned as he moved against her, holding her to his hardening body with increased desire. "Crissy . . . baby," he breathed into her mouth, reluctant to leave the warmth of her lips. "Trust me. I would never hurt you, honey," he promised, kissing her again and again and again, feeling her complete surrender in his arms. "Come home with me," he begged, breathing raggedly now. "I want to love you . . . so much." His words surprised even him. He hadn't intended to say any such thing. A man of his experience knew better. But, damn, this woman felt so good in his arms. So soft and yielding. He couldn't deny that his words expressed his exact desire. He wanted her . . . perhaps forever.

His words were like a dash of cold lake water on her senses, and she reeled, and stumbled away from his arms. "No, no." She groaned. "I'm going to *my* home," she whispered, suddenly feeling the chill of the night coupled with the desolation of her escape from his strong arms. Without a word, he led her back to the car.

When he got in himself, he took the top of the steering wheel in his hands and leaned his head on them. "I apologize, Crissy," he said in a low, contrite voice. "I rushed you . . . and that's *all* I'm apologizing for. I've never met anyone like you. You've got to believe me. *This is no line!* But I'm afraid my baser instincts took over my good intentions . . . *especially* when you kissed me back," he reminded her in a rather gruff voice. "I just can't seem to get enough of you, honey," he ended, cursing himself for ruining the evening and wondering if he'd destroyed his chances.

His obvious discomfort struck a responsive chord in Crissy's heart. She couldn't let him go without explaining her actions to him. In this she had to be truthful. She reached over and smoothed his silky hair. And when he raised his head to look at her with a questioning and somewhat hopeful expression, she could not deny she was falling in love with him. "I owe you an apology, too, James," she began softly, feeling his eyes burn into hers. "The truth is, where you're concerned, I have a rather difficult time refusing. But you've got to understand. Although I've dated a great deal since I lost my husband, I've never found myself in a position where I didn't *want* to refuse. I need more time, James. I've never had an affair, and I'm not sure I could handle it. Quite honestly, it's never come up before," she ended with a sigh.

"You're not angry, then?"

"No."

"Then, spend tomorrow with me. Prove to me you're not going to disappear again, Crissy. Let me take you out to the lake to see my new home."

Tomorrow was her day off. Why not spend part of it with him? She smiled tremulously, and replied, "I'd like that very much, James. You can call me in the morning and we'll work out the details, okay?"

He kissed her exuberantly on the mouth and grinned from ear to ear. "We'll have a marvelous time. You'll see, honey," he promised, pulling out a business card and a pen to take down her number. The drive back to the restaurant was filled with happy, relaxed conversation and teasing humor. When he walked her to her car, he kissed her warmly, but without deep passion, holding himself in firm control. "Are you sure you won't let me follow you home, Crissy?" he asked again. The smoldering light in his eyes let her know he was aware of her continued mistrust of him as an outsider.

She acknowledged his look of consternation and let Tulip speak for her. "Jimmy Bob, you'd shore nuf git lost ifen you follered me to my little cabin. Why, honey, we might not find yo'all for days and days. Could be a pole cat might decide to have you fer breakfast," she teased.

Silently he helped her into her car and leaned over to kiss her on the forehead. "Go home, Tulip . . . get a good night's rest. . . ." Then he dropped his mouth to cover hers in an overpowering kiss that absolutely stole the breath from her body. "And Tulip, remember—tomorrow is your day off. Stay home when Crissy comes to my house," he ordered, his cautioning words prompting Crissy to say good night in her own voice. He stood in the parking lot, watching as she drove her little red car down the street.

She still felt breathless when she arrived at her cottage in the woods. For a moment she sat in the parked car and relived the feel of his mouth on hers. Shivering in anticipation of their plans for tomorrow, she hoped he might begin truly to care for her. "It would be so nice to have someone to love who loved me back." She sighed, getting out of her car and looking up at the countless stars overhead. "I'm so tired of being alone," she said to the wind. "So tired." In a short time she was snuggled beneath the smooth, cool sheets, and her body entered a dream-filled state where she and James danced to the throbbing beat of jungle drums until they collapsed, in their passion, onto a white sand beach.

Four

She awoke the next morning refreshed and eager for her day's activities with James. At nine o'clock the phone rang. She nervously picked up the receiver, but instead of simply saying hello, she repeated the last four digits of her phone number, using a completely different voice—one she knew sounded like an answering service. She had been doing this for years, and no one, except Katie, in New York, knew her secret. It was just another way to protect herself. "Five two one two," she recited in a rather nasal tone. "May I help you?"

For a moment there was no sound on the other end of the line. "Yes," she prodded. "May I help you?" she asked again in her answering-service voice.

"Ah, is this the number where I can reach Ms. Crissy Brant?" said a low familiar voice that sent heat waves down Crissy's spine and brought an impish smile to her face. "One moment, pul-ease," she told him, and put the phone on hold. Then she released the button and said in her own voice, "Crissy Brant here."

"Getting you to part with your telephone number didn't help me a bit, did it?" he complained.

"Good morning to you too," she replied, laughing at his inability to cover his frustration at his discovery. She told him that sometimes she used the answering service and sometimes she simply put her phone on her own answering device. "It just depends on Carrie's whims," she fantasized, telling him the woman who ran the answering service wasn't always available. "What shall we do today?" she asked to get him off the subject of her phone idiosyncrasies.

"I have two errands to run this morning, honey, so I'm planning on meeting you at the Wooden Nickle parking lot at noon," he said. "If by any chance you're disappointed that we can't spend the morning together as well, I'll lessen the pain by telling you that both errands involve surprises for you."

"For me?" she squealed into the receiver. "How did you know I love surprises, James?"

He chuckled in his low, vibrant voice. "Just a hunch," he replied. "Our time together will begin with a marvelous picnic on my patio, followed by a game of tennis and then a cooling swim . . . not necessarily in that order. Wear your tennis outfit, but don't forget to bring your swimming suit and a change of clothes for this evening, because we're going to barbecue for supper," he informed her.

"I hadn't planned on spending the evening with you, James," she said hesitantly. "I told you I need some time to think," she reminded him.

"Think tomorrow, honey," he replied, laughing. "Today is strictly for fun . . . and games!" After a moment he asked, as if he had a sudden thought, "You don't have other plans for tonight, do you?" His voice relaxed again when she told him her only plans included him. "Good! Then, get ready to meet me at noon, Crissy. I can't wait to show you your surprises."

She laughed, too, joining into the spirit of the warm, sunny day. "You just said the magic word," she admitted, her smile showing right through her voice. "See you at noon."

She was sitting on her bed, her arms wrapped around her robe-covered body; she was giddy with happiness, wondering what James had thought up for her surprises. Then she snapped her fingers in agitation, remembering that she had wanted to call Tom Sinclair last night. "Darn," she said, "I wonder if I can reach him at work."

She called New York information and got his new office number, saying a silent prayer, as she dialed, that he would be in his office. After one delay while her call was being transferred, she heard her friend's cordial voice on the line. "Tom Sinclair here," he said, but was immediately his jovial, teasing self when Crissy identified herself. "Belle," he exclaimed, using the name she went by in the advertising world. "How are you, way out there in the sticks, my friend? Met any interesting tourists lately?" he teased. It was his ongoing joke with her.

He was surprised when she answered, "As a matter of fact, I have, Tom." But the man was completely floored when she told him she had met Mr. James Robert Prince III.

"My God, Belle," he crowed. "He's almost my brother-in-law!"

"I know, Tom. That's why I'm calling you," she replied succinctly. She told him she had no idea how long she was going to go on seeing him, "but I find him interesting—"

"And a challenge," he interrupted. "Right?"

She laughed softly. "And that too," she admitted. "The point is this. If, sometime in the future, we chance to meet in his presence, you must promise to keep my identity a secret. He knows nothing about my commercial work . . . and I'm not ready yet to tell him everything about myself," she explained. "We've only been on two dates, and I have no idea what his feelings about me might be. If I decided not to see him anymore, he might be able to use that information against me in some way."

"I'll bet you've been talking to our old friend Katie," he guessed. "And I get the distinct impression you don't trust James. Does that about sum it up?"

"He does have quite a reputation, Tom," she said, defending her decision.

"And not wholly unwarranted, I'll admit, Belle, but he's a lot deeper than you might imagine."

"You may be a bit prejudiced," she replied, gently accusing. "After all, you love his sister."

"Now, *that's* a fact!" he answered, laughing happily. "If you know about Julie and me, then, you know what her profession is, right?"

"Yes."

"But did James tell you he completely financed her education and contributes heavily to her lab so she can continue with her work? She's very close to a breakthrough now," he informed her.

When she did not at once confirm the information, he laughed triumphantly. "No, I didn't think he would tell you about *that*! He's really a very fine man, Belle. Give him a chance. Get to know him before you decide he's an unfeeling playboy. I know for a fact, he would never break a confidence. But, yes, I promise, should we meet when he's around I'll continue to keep your identity a secret if you haven't chosen to share that information with him. Now, anything else, honey?"

"No, Tom," she answered. "Thanks for your time . . . and best of luck in your coming marriage. I hope you'll be very happy."

"If I can get that woman of mine out of her lab and down the aisle, I'll consider myself some kind of miracle worker." He chortled happily. "And I wish you the same, honey." Then he was gone, and Crissy was left with the impression he knew something she didn't.

Crissy was humming merrily when she pulled alongside James's car in the parking lot. "Hi," she greeted him jauntily, taking the hand he offered to her. "It's a beautiful day for a picnic," she remarked, feeling a little self-conscious standing in front of him.

His grip tightened momentarily on her fingers when his warm gaze wandered caressingly along her short white tennis dress. He whistled low and long, a definite Brooklyn wolf-whistle. "Baby, you could stop traffic on Fifth Avenue," he crooned appreciatively. "I've never seen such long legs," he went on, embarrassing Crissy. "If you ever get tired of teaching, I can make you a top New York model," he continued. Then, "On second thought, cancel that offer. I'd be jealous as hell, having other men look at you . . . I want you *all* for myself, honey," he said, smiling wickedly as he noted with masculine pleasure the heightened color in her cheeks. "Come on, let's get your stuff and hit the road."

Inside the car, he leaned over and kissed her warmly. "Hi, sweetheart," he said in a low, husky voice, kissing the tip of her nose for good measure. When he got back onto the highway he grumbled in exasperation, "I'm going to have to buy a new car. I can't even hold your hand while we're driving. I have to keep shifting down for these damn hills."

"Maybe I can help you out. You do the driving and I'll do the shifting." She moved as far to the left as the car would allow, continuing to hold his hand, which he brought over to his hard, muscled thigh; with her right hand she shifted gears with professional ability. "See, every problem has a solution. You just have to find it, that's all," she instructed, sounding like someone teaching positive thinking.

"You're something else," he said with smiling approval. "I think I'm going to keep you, baby," he told her, adding sternly before she had a chance to deny his wish, "Shift!" And she did.

Five miles out of town, along a peninsula jutting out like a curved finger into Table Rock Lake, James stopped the car in front of a heavy, wrought-iron gate barring the entrance to his property. Quickly he unlocked the padlock and swung the gate open. When he got back into the car, he smiled shyly at Crissy. "That's not for the home folk," he explained. "It's for the outsiders!"

His land was typical mountain terrain—low mountains, actually—but the road wound around and through the hills and valleys, giving Crissy a chance to reaffirm the rightness of her decision to come back to her home in these hills. The meadow grasses were still green, and undulated in the gentle breeze. The pine trees grew straight and tall, reaching for the bright blue, cloudless sky above, and song birds twittered among the profuse, colorful wild flowers, while a gray rabbit scampered for shelter to escape the talons of a hawk circling over its head. She sighed contentedly as she watched the play of nature's gifts upon the landscape.

"There's something you don't see on Madison Avenue," James said, interrupting her reverie when he pointed out a white-tailed doe at the edge of the forest.

"At least, not the four-legged variety," Crissy couldn't resist qualifying.

"Point taken!" He laughed softly as he ordered her to shift. "You know, I never realized dual driving could be so much fun." He pulled her free hand to rub her palm over his lips, his moustache tickling her flesh, and then down onto his hard, warm chest, causing her to grind the gear box mercilessly. He chuckled at her disconcerted "Oh, damn!," adding, "But we're going to have to work on your concentration, Crissy, my girl."

Not to be outdone, she stuck her tongue out at him in a childish gesture of revolt. They drove through a deeply shadowed grove of trees and then they were approaching a breathtakingly beautiful lakeside home. Except for some additional landscaping, it appeared as if the house were ready for occupancy, and when Crissy voiced the thought, James stopped the car in the driveway and told her quietly, "I moved in three days ago. You're the first person I've invited to my new home, Crissy. Welcome!" He kissed her softly on her warm mouth. Their eyes locked momentarily, and his carried the sincerity of his welcome, while hers showed her somewhat confused but heartfelt response. "Come on, honey," he said, and they climbed out of the car and strode, hand in hand, away from the building in order to turn and see its splendor all at once.

His home was a one-story structure constructed of native stone and cedar siding. The peaked roof was covered in shake shingles and blended with the other natural materials. James led her around the side of the rambling house, informing her that he had designed it himself, and Crissy was once again impressed with his diverse abilities. At the back of the house she couldn't help but exclaim over the spacious patio made from slabs of granite set into a bed of white sand. But the feature that simply took her breath away was the large rectangular sparkling pool that extended several yards from the back of the house and flowed beneath an immense glass wall into the living room beyond.

"The glass wall extends to the bottom of the pool when it gets cold," he explained. "We'll be able to swim all winter. The glass will allow the sun to provide a great deal of heat for the water, but the pool has a separate heater too," he went on. "I always wanted a year-round pool . . . and now I've got one."

Crissy had not overlooked the fact that he had said, "*We'll* swim all winter," but she simply could not burst his bubble of happiness in showing her his home. "It's simply breathtaking, James," was all she said.

He grabbed her hand and led her to the outdoor cooking area at the edge of the patio. "See, this is the built-in gas barbecue we're going to christen tonight. Isn't it great?" he exclaimed enthusiastically. "I won't have to get all messed up with charcoal dust every time I want to make us a meal."

Again, he had used the plural, but Crissy ignored the implied message, matching his long strides as he took her along to the lakeshore. He doesn't mean a thing by it, she told herself. He's just using the administrative "we," so don't read anything into it! The view from the quiet inlet was spectacular. The water was clear and smooth, protected from the buffeting winds coming across the great expanse of the open lake. The beach reflected with snowy brilliance the sun's neon glare. And when she looked out over the water, she saw the forested hills and peaceful scene before her.

She breathed the fresh, unpolluted air and visibly relaxed, a feeling of calmness flowing through her body. "You have a beautiful home, James," she whispered, almost as if she should not raise her voice to disturb the stillness around her.

Gently he took her face in his large hands and traced her features, finally caressing her trembling lips with his thumbs. His eyes penetrated to her very soul. He'll read my mind, Crissy thought in despair. But her gaze must have revealed only her rising panic, because he slowly leaned forward and kissed her tenderly, carefully nurturing her senses until she began to relax again. "Could you be happy living here, sweetheart?" he murmured, continuing to hold her with his fingertips.

The panic rose into her throat like a fist. She tried to laugh off his question. "What woman wouldn't give her heart and soul to live in a place like this?" she exclaimed, breathless in her attempt to break his spell.

He did not release his hold, but Crissy watched nervously as she spotted the hard muscle clench in his strong jaw. "I wasn't talking about *any* woman, Crissy," he continued in a low tone of voice that now seemed laced with fury. "But you're right about one thing . . . it *would* cost you your heart and soul!" He brought his mouth back to hers.

She whimpered against his opened, demanding mouth, feeling the heat of her traitorous body flow into his. Her hands fluttered at her sides as she continued to moan, fighting her own reactions to his sensual, slow determination to break down her meager defenses. "Kiss me, Crissy," he murmured insistently. "Give me *that,* at least." He pushed his right hand to the back of her neck to hold her head still while his other hand dropped to her rounded bottom to lift her hips into his rising need.

The battle between her brain and her body was short-lived, and she slipped her arms around his waist to meld against his insistent length. Her response was simultaneously punctuated by her moan of surrender and his groan of satisfaction. The kiss they shared began to deepen in intensity; for the moment both James and Crissy were given only to the sensations of delight and experimentation as she opened her mouth to his thrusting tongue and accepted the inevitable. He would take her right here—she could not fight herself or him any longer. She wanted him with every screaming, throbbing cell in her body.

Slowly he lowered her onto the grassy hillside, continuing his erotic magic inside her mouth. His increasingly ragged breathing showed how much he welcomed her counter moves as she insisted on exploring his mouth with her hot tongue and nipped and sucked deliriously on his wet lips. Half afraid of breaking the spell, she gently pushed eager fingers through his thick brown hair and opened her eyes to his fiery gaze.

His hot breath washed over her tingling, flushed face when she boldly slid her hands to his shoulders and pulled him down on her reclining body, sighing when she felt his weight press her into the tender grasses. The effect of their embrace was like a bolt of blue lightening igniting their souls. His kiss was molten fire, searing her mouth with awesome effect until she was weak with longing. He crushed her to him with such force that she had no more breath to continue and she began to feel light-headed as he sucked the very life-force from her body.

She would not, could not, signal the end to the most passionate kiss she had experienced in her entire life! She'd just die here in his arms, she thought melodramatically . . . until she found she could breathe again because he had released her mouth and begun the torturous journey to her breasts, which had somehow become uncovered for his touch. The heavy feeling there increased when he lowered his head to the already hard rosy tips. And when his lips and tongue explored in circles of heat, only to fasten like a greedy infant around first one and then the other nipple, Crissy could contain the sensation no longer. She moaned in tortured arousal, trying feverishly to unbutton his shirt and crying out in anguish at her interrupted attempts when he began to use his hands to caress and massage her body in tandem with his seeking, willful mouth.

"Help me!" she pleaded. "I can't stand it," she cried, once again working at the buttons of his shirt.

James pulled a little away from her writhing inviting body and gasped, "Neither can I, baby. Neither can I!" His breathing continued to come in ragged gasps as his eyes drank their fill of her voluptuous tanned body. He moved his gaze to her face and watched the dark, chaotic emotions mirrored in her smoky eyes and love-swollen soft mouth. "You're the most beautiful woman in the world," he whispered. "I never wanted to make love more than I do at this moment . . . but I'm not going to give in!" He smiled poignantly at the confusion in her eyes. "No, I'm following my intuition now, and my intuition tells me this is *not* the time to make love . . . at least the way I want to make love to *you*."

"I don't understand." Crissy whimpered, feeling the wild beating of her heart against her throbbing, awakened breasts. "I want you too," she admitted softly, her voice filled with a desire that matched the message rising from her half-closed eyes.

James drew a shuddering, tortured breath into his lungs, fighting for control when he heard the passionate murmured words. He actually believed he could feel the heat of her invitation rise up to caress his skin. But he succeeded in ruling his aching need, and with shaking fingers he refastened her bra over her firm breasts, closing his eyes against the vision but seeing it still, branded forever in his brain. He fought to complete his self-appointed task of buttoning her blouse, and even tried to shut his ears against the sound of her harsh breathing. Finally he pulled her to a sitting position next to him and turned her so he could look into her eyes.

"You didn't want me in the beginning, Crissy," he reminded her. "I took advantage of you and tried my damnedest to break down that wall around you."

She smiled shyly, her eyes telling the full story. "You succeeded very quickly, James," she whispered throatily.

"But the fact remains, you had to be kissed into submission," he countered in a gruff voice, his struggle against his own needs not yet over. "I want more than your body . . . I want *all* of you." His tone was determined. "I want your body, your heart, *and* your soul, honey. I *need* all of you . . . and I'm just bullheaded enough to refuse anything less." He caressed her cheek gently. "Do you understand? *Can* you understand? This is an all-or-nothing situation. In every important step in my life, I've always fallen back on that concept. I'll work like hell to win . . . but I want it all . . . or I want nothing!"

Oh, she understood him perfectly. *He* wanted her to come to him with her heart and soul wrapped up in her willing, passionate body and served to him on a platter. But he hadn't said the words *she* needed to hear. Did he love her? Could he love her as deeply as she felt she was falling in love with him? Did he want to spend the rest of his life with her? Did he want to marry her and give her children? Or would he tire of her and drop her surrendered package of love into the nearest trash bin when he found someone more interesting? God, she didn't know what to say. Well, when in doubt, make 'em laugh, she lectured herself.

Looking at him with a very serious face but showing the spark of laughter in her eyes, she gravely observed, "I'll bet you're a helluva poker player!"

He shook his head sadly and chuckled in a deprecating tone. Sighing, he asked, "Oh, Crissy, why do you keep running away?" Then he lifted himself to his feet in one smooth motion and reached down to pull her up. "You say you wanna see some cutthroat competition? You say you wanna see *mean*?" he chanted like an old-time carnival barker. "Tell you what I'm gon-na do. I'm gonna take you now to the newly completed tennis court and . . . knock your socks off!" he promised, dragging her across the lawn to the other side of the house.

"I'm not wearing any socks."

"Then, I'll just knock some sense *into* you," he shot back, revealing more about the upcoming game than he should have.

"Them's fightin' words," challenged Tulip, her will to win erupting in that statement to give strength to the phrase.

He halted, and they stood toe to toe, their eyes snapping, their bodies stiff with suppressed desires. There was barely a hand's breadth between their tense faces when he hissed, "A fight to the death, right?"

"Right!" she hissed back, but he did not release his iron grip on her hand when they ran to the new clay court. At the side stood a small cedar building, where he stored the equipment. He slipped inside, handed her two rackets and cans of balls, and instructed her to go over to the court to warm up while he changed into his shorts. A few minutes later James emerged in his tennis whites and jogged to the sideline to snatch up his racket and stick two tennis balls into his pocket. Crissy was so intent on admiring *his* long muscular legs that she only heard the whistle of his first serve when it whizzed by her.

"Point!" he shouted fiercely, and fired another ball over the net, which almost knocked her down with its force when she returned it to his court. He was so surprised when she managed to hit his second serve that he overreacted and watched with dismay as the ball bounced far behind her, out of bounds.

They screamed and yelled over rules and line balls, using enough energy to propel a dozen players around the court. Crissy held her own against his powerful backhand, making every shot count as she used placement to her advantage. Finally the score was tied one-all, and James moved in for the kill on match point. Crissy dug deep into her reserves for the last bit of strength left in her body. It wasn't enough. And when he won, he leaped over the net like a frisky gazelle and swung her around in his arms, kissing her soundly on her moist mouth.

"What a game!" he exclaimed, a wide grin on his flushed face. "You're a real tiger on the court, woman!" When he saw she wasn't smiling, he prodded, "Aren't you going to congratulate me, Crissy?"

She muttered her faint praise for his fine game, then added sulkily, "I was hoping I would beat *you.*"

He took her racket from her bruised little hand and began to walk her back to the house. "Well, at least we have that in common. We both like to win," he replied, dropping the equipment at the storage building and bringing a towel back with him to mop their wet faces and arms. He left her in one of the reclining chairs in the shade of the patio and went into the house to get their lunch. "Promise you won't come after me, Crissy," he insisted. "If you do, you'll ruin one of my surprises."

She told him she didn't think she would be able to move for a week and waved him away so she could rest in peace. In ten minutes he was back, pushing a cherry-wood tea cart laden with appetizing cold cuts, aged cheeses, and refreshing fruit and vegetable finger foods. Thick wedges of bread were on another plate, and beside it was a large crystal pitcher of lemonade, the ice gently tinkling against the sides as he moved the cart across the patio. After they had eaten their fill, they rested on their chaises for perhaps half an hour, and then James reached over to get a tiny box that was hidden in the corner of the cart.

He handed it to Crissy, who looked at it with sleepy eyes, wondering what was in it. "You'll have to open it, honey," he chided gently, smiling at her childlike expression. "It's your first surprise . . . the one I promised you last night to replace the red silk scarf."

She was smiling in anticipation now. It was obviously a jeweler's box, but she gasped with genuine surprise when she lifted the lid. Resting on white velvet was a delicate ruby tulip charm suspended on a fine gold chain. "Oh, James, it's exquisite," she exclaimed softly, holding it up so they both could see. "I've never seen anything like it."

"I hope *not,*" he responded. "I was promised it was one of a kind, Crissy . . . for a one of a kind woman. Would you like me to put it on for you?" he offered. "I realize you're already wearing red," he observed, pinching the toe of her red tennis shoe, "but this is something you can wear all the time . . . just in case you someday forget your trademark," he added, coming around to her back and fastening the clasp at her neck. Then he bent and kissed the soft skin beneath her ear, making her shudder and get goose bumps all along her arms.

"Don't!" she burst out, jumping up to get away from his touch. Struggling to recapture control of her senses, she gave an excuse for her behavior that was true, but glossed over the real reason. "I feel all hot and sticky, James. I'd like to freshen up, if you don't mind."

He pulled her red silk scarf from his pocket and gave her a devilish grin in preparation for his last surprise. "I'll take you inside so you can shower before we go swimming." He laughed at his words. "God, that sounds inane, doesn't it? Well, at least redundant." He chuckled. "But, little Crissy, you'll have to let me blindfold you if you want to get inside. The other surprise has to be set up. Are you game?" He lifted the scarf toward her face.

She held up her hand, touching his wrist, giving herself another electric shock that surprised her with its intensity. Good Lord, she couldn't even touch him! To James she retorted, "You're asking quite a lot from me on faith alone. How do I know you won't walk me right into the pool, over there?"

His brilliant, sky-blue gaze tangled with hers, and he murmured, "Trust me."

"Do you promise?"

All he replied was, "Trust me!" Crissy mumbled her agreement, full of reservations but also with a deeper sense that James was asking for her confidence in more than this one playful act. He was "working like hell," as he had put it in plain words, to win her trust and confidence. It seemed to be a very important step for him, although Crissy still felt as if it were only being used as a ploy so he could eventually get what he wanted.

Quickly he tied the scarf over her eyes and stepped in front of her to take her hands, leading her toward the back entrance of the house, which was sheltered by some low shrubbery and a wide, latticework outer wall. He cautioned her to take one small step up into the enclosure and moved her back against its wall. "Don't move, Crissy," he ordered softly. "Get ready for your surprise," he whispered, removing the scarf from her face.

She stood very still and slowly opened her eyes, looking straight ahead at the door. The sight that filled her line of vision was so overwhelming that tears at once flooded down her cheeks, for there, before her, was her favorite piece from the wood carver's exhibit—the carved door with the redbird art-glass-window inset. "Oh, James! It's so beautiful. But how did you get it installed so quickly?" She gazed at the vibrant color of the cardinal as she ran her fingers lovingly over the carved mountain scene below.

James had moved to the side when he removed her blindfold, and was watching her reaction with something akin to absolute pleasure. "It was one of the errands I did this morning, after some almost predawn phone calls. When I went to pay for it, I gave them a key, and they were kind enough to bring it right over and install it," he explained. "The question I want answered is—does it *really* please you?"

She turned to him and smiled through her tears of joyful surprise. "Does it please me?" she parroted. "Do you even have to ask? Look at me. I'm crying like a baby." She scrubbed at her face with the backs of her hands. She didn't quite understand why her approval was of such great importance to him. "I'm so glad you chose it for yourself, James. Every morning the sun will flood the art glass with light. Even when it's raining, you can flip on the outside light and you'll have your redbird companion," she added, glancing at the spotlight above her head. "It will give you so much pleasure, James."

He drew her into his arms and looked lovingly into her heavily lashed, glittering eyes. "The pleasure will be that I'll always think of you—every time I look at that redbird—and, probably, every time I see *anything* red." He bent his head to kiss her, and the touch of his lips was so gentle, filled with such warmth and tenderness, that Crissy could only wrap her arms around him to try to capture the feeling forever in her heart. When the kiss ended, they both sighed as they leaned against each other, their foreheads touching. "Welcome home, sweetheart," he murmured, and pushed the door open for her entrance.

She jerked her head up and stared, wide-eyed, at James. But the shutter had closed over his tender emotions. He grinned and gave her a little shove into the kitchen, scolding jovially, "Well, are you going in or not?"

She scooted through the door and then stood in the center of the pegged oak floor, looking about her with genuine interest. It was an old-fashioned room. Handsome oak cabinets with black wrought-iron hinges and handles lined two walls. At the large picture window, where one could look out on the lakeshore and hills beyond, sat a round oak table, surrounded by four comfortable-looking bentwood armchairs. Bright red cushions were on each chair and accented the other uses of red in the room. The colors in the red-and-white gingham café curtains were repeated in the scalloped trim around the top of the walls, which were painted with white enamel. Even the dinnerware, James pointed out, was white china with red and gold stripes around the edge. On the other two walls he had hung several different-sized oak-framed colored photographs of old-time processed fruits and vegetables. There was one of onions drying on a long hemp cord, another showed a huge handwoven basket overflowing with shiny red apples, and a third pictured a still-life composition of potatoes, yellow squash and purple cabbage. James had taken the photographs, although he was shy about admitting it. The decor was impressive, and Crissy was lavish with her praise of his good taste.

"Don't give me all the credit, honey," he remarked, happy at her reaction. "I have a very good interior decorator. I told her what I wanted—what I saw for each room—and she did all the buying and took care of the details. I'm just stuck with the bills!" He grinned now because he saw the alert look in Crissy's eyes when he spoke of his decorator. "Her name is Angela Layton, and she's one of the top decorators on the East Coast," he volunteered. "We've known one another for a long time. I really played on our friendship to convince her to fly here into the 'outback,' as she calls it, to decorate this place." Crissy made no comment, and James goaded teasingly, "Aren't you just a little bit jealous, honey?"

She turned a righteous glare on him, replying indignantly, "Certainly not!" But somehow that strange pain she'd felt the night before, gathered around her heart again.

"Foiled again," he mumbled plaintively, and took her hand for a tour of the rest of the house. Off the kitchen was his combination study and office. The room was lined with floor-to-ceiling walnut shelves filled with books. Dominating the sparse, businesslike decor was a handsome carved antique desk and oversized executive chair, which swiveled around for when James wanted to think or rest, looking out the huge picture window onto the sylvan scene outdoors. Two old-fashioned oak filing cabinets stood side by side against another wall. They had been refinished with loving care, and Crissy was not surprised to learn that James had done this too. There was one glaringly modern convenience, a high-technology computer and word processor, standing in the corner on another antique wooden table. Crissy smiled when she walked over to the sleek computer, quipping, "I see you can't get by without some newfangled machinery."

"It's of great use to me in my business," he answered almost apologetically. "This is the twentieth century, Crissy. Today's commerce doesn't exist in a dream world, honey. I need all the help I can get."

"At the school where I teach, they've installed several different types of computers for classroom use," Crissy remarked. "Two of my students won scholarships for their advanced programming skills last year. I was so proud of them."

"You've got computers in your little mountain school?" he asked in disbelief.

She bridled at his comment, then remembered she had not told him where she really worked. Still, she took a fighting stance, putting her feet apart and planting her tight little fists on her rounded hips. "My dear Mr. Prince, even in these hills we no longer have a backwoods mentality," she told him with a fierce pride of her people evident in her strident voice. "That's only window dressing for the tourists," she told him. "They love it, but many are not aware that a large chunk of the money they leave in these mountains has helped to finance our children's education."

He moved toward her with silent grace, but a wicked light was gleaming in his clear blue eyes. "You're gorgeous when you get mad," he crooned sensuously. "I love it when you get on your soapbox and start yelling."

"*I was not yell—*" she tried to object, but he had led her right down the path, taking full advantage of her parted lips to kiss her with such authority and passion, she was unable to stifle the moan of pleasure that erupted into his mouth, vibrating against his warm purposeful lips. Her legs turned to jelly, and she would have fallen at his feet if his arms had not tightened around her waist, finally moving to her rounded hips to pull her against him. She trembled under his devastating touch. His mouth and darting tongue continued to plunder and duel with hers. When she moaned again in her rising passion, he growled his approval and lifted one hand to her thrusting, firm breast, fondling and caressing her feminine softness with a fiery touch.

But he gently pushed her away. He shook his head self-consciously when he looked down at her glazed eyes. "I love it even *more* when you surrender." He sighed. "Too much!" he conceded gruffly. He loosened his hold on her body, not completely setting her free, as if he knew she'd fall in a heap on the braided rug if he did. Taking a deep breath, he muttered, morosely, "I did it again. Damn! I can't believe it."

Crissy still could not find enough sense in her head to question him, but her face was an open book, and he read her thought. "I can't keep my hands off you, Crissy Brant," he told her, as if that would explain his actions. Then a thoughtful, dreamy look crossed his handsome features. "Mmmm, I wonder what it would be like if you couldn't keep your hands off *me*." His low voice was husky with desire. His eyes smoldered with sensual messages. But he did not touch her.

Quickly she stepped away from the heat of his tall body. She had to move or he was going to find out, she thought, vexed. He's going to keep fighting his feelings until I come to him *first*. She knew it with every fiber of her body . . . and her soul . . . and, dammit, with her heart! She glanced over her shoulder when she heard him chuckling, low and warm, knowing exactly how his words had affected her. She gave his smiling face a cutting glance. "Let's complete the tour, shall we?" He didn't refuse.

The living room was completely different from the part of the house she had seen so far. It was huge and informal, with great deep sofas of white arranged into a conversation pit before the fireplace; large tropical plants in tubs gave vibrant green beauty to spots throughout the room. A game table was in one corner, and in the other was an expensive audiovisual center, with all its components housed in a built-in unit. The focal point was, of course, the sparkling blue pool. The sun's rays through the glass wall mirrored the water images into undulating shapes around the room and onto the high, vaulted ceiling. Crissy was drawn to the water like one hypnotized by its shimmering invitation. James walked over and quietly leaned down to dip his fingers into the water, testing its temperature.

"Good," he proclaimed proudly. "It's warm. Would you mind if we christened the pool today rather than swimming in the lake?" he asked, rising to stand at her side. "I was experimenting with the controls last night, trying to find the setting that would combine optimally with the solar heat. Looks like I found it, because the water is just right. Okay with you, honey?"

"The lake gets a little chilly this late in the season," she admitted. "But I'd like to see the rest of the house first, if you don't mind."

"We're on our way, little lady." He took her arm and formally swept his hand to the side. "Right this way."

Down a wide hallway to the other side of the house, he showed her a cozy pecan-paneled den with a comfortable leather couch and two chairs situated in front of a handsome stone fireplace. "It'll be a nice place to hole up on cold winter evenings, don't you think?" She nodded in agreement and felt another surge of heat curl down to her toes.

Then he guided her to the bedrooms, three in all. Two were done in contrasting earth tones, one using the darker shades as the dominant color and the other relying upon the lighter tones, but she was unprepared for the master bedroom when he opened the heavy carved door for her. It was a very large room and had an airy appearance, with the bright afternoon sun flooding through one glass wall. The whole room was done in eggshell white—the walls, the drapes, the thick carpeting, and the intricately quilted cover for the huge four-poster cherry-wood bedstead, which matched the other massive furnishings in the room. The glow of the satiny wood furniture with heavy brass fittings gave warmth to the otherwise austere room.

"It's a lovely room," she said aloud, but her heart prodded her to utter very different words: I could be happy here. So happy.

"I'm glad you like it, Crissy," he said, rather formally. "Look, you go ahead and start your shower and I'll run out to the car and get your bag," he suggested, already turning toward the open door and effectively breaking the electric mood.

She slipped into the bathroom, which was majestic in its splendor, with gold fixtures and a huge marble tub. "I'll say this for the man. He goes first class." She chuckled, locking the door and undressing quickly. She was under the warm pulsating spray when there was a hard knock on the door and she heard James shout over the noise of the shower. "I'll leave your bag right outside the door, Crissy. I'll use the other shower . . . to save time," he grumbled, bringing an impish smile to her lips, since she wagered he would much rather be in there with her.

In a short time she had washed the perspiration from her slim, tanned body and shampooed her hair, thinking at the time that it was rather a silly thing to do, but wanting to rid herself of the aftereffects of her challenging tennis match. She stealthily opened the bathroom door and found her bag, just as James had promised. Hurriedly she put on her red bikini, wishing it covered more than it did. Then, throwing her hip-length white coverup over her suit, she walked barefoot to the indoor pool.

When she arrived, James was standing at the side of the pool waiting for her. His hands were draped carelessly on his hips, which were covered by black racing trunks. The sun glinted off the gold streaks in his damp, wavy hair and his tanned, Adonis form shimmered with the pool's reflection. Crissy halted several feet away from him and was unaware of the hungry look that came into her dark eyes. She stood very still, feeling her heart hammer against her chest, and visually devoured and memorized his rippling muscles. She followed from shoulder to ankle his contours, wanted suddenly to trace her fingers along the pathway of golden hair that covered his chest, disappeared beneath the tight black trunks, and continued along his well-developed legs. Finally she tore her eyes away and lifted her gaze to meet his eyes. He had the aura of a jungle beast getting ready to pounce. Then a little smile pulled at her lips, and she filled the room with a piercing, low whistle of approval, bringing a flush of pleasure and confusion to his face.

"Hey," he murmured complimentarily when she threw her short robe on the thick green rug and hesitated before she walked to the pool. "That's my line. My God," he rumbled deep in his broad, hair-matted chest, "Heaven trimmed in a red bikini! I must be in Paradise." He gasped, still in shock when he continued to discover and assimilate the beauty of her figure.

"Well, it's just my trademark," she reminded him shyly, slipping into the water and floating languidly upon the surface.

"And *what* a trademark!" he declared, feeling at a distinct disadvantage standing at the side of the pool, completely unable to control his arousal as he watched her. "Do you have your life-saving badge?" he asked in a harsh voice.

Puzzled, she pulled her feet to the bottom of the pool and stood up in the waist-deep warm water. "As a matter of fact, I do. Why?"

"At the moment I don't feel particularly well coordinated," he grumbled, getting ready to dive but still unable to pull his eyes away from her voluptuous body, wet and sleek.

She giggled, suddenly aware of the root of his troubles, and contradicted slyly, "You look rather 'well coordinated' to me!"

"That comment hit below the belt," he muttered. His eyes snapped at her now.

She lay back into the caressing waters and floated away, murmuring erotically through curved lips, "It certainly does!" Swimming well out of his reach, she tossed back, using Tulip's voice, "Come on, city feller, I reckon yore not half sweet enuf to melt."

"That does it!" He made a clean dive into the deep end of the pool and swam underwater until he could grab her. But she was a good swimmer, and slipped away from his grasp at the last moment, dodging his many attempts to catch her. The playful game went on for several minutes, with much shouting and many dares thrown back and forth across the churning pool. Crissy was having so much fun outfoxing James that she failed to realize he was moving her into the deepest part of the pool and finally had her cornered. Through narrowed eyes he watched her growing awareness that she was caught in his trap.

She laughed nervously, wondering if she had subconsciously cooperated in his planned snare. "Well, what are you going to do now?" Her eyes moved slowly over his body, revealing a sensuous awareness of his form.

He took a deep, shuddering breath, expanding his glistening chest to eye-popping proportions, and smiled stoically. His eyes still measured her reaction to his movement. "I'm not going to do a thing, Crissy . . . not a damn thing," he ground out between the clenched teeth of his artificial and pained smile. His moustache twitched. He took off for the opposite end of the pool, diving neatly beneath the elevated glass wall to the outside. She was left alone to ponder his sudden change of tactics . . . *again.*

"That man!" she seethed, feeling the throbbing ache that was growing in her loins. "Now what's he up to?" She swam in a fury to join him.

James was terribly urbane in his conversation for the rest of their swim, which they divided between both ends of the pool. He never touched her in anything but an accidental manner and then glided away from her to swim on.

An hour later, when the sun was beginning its descent toward evening, he sneaked up behind her and lifted a squealing Crissy out of the water to the smooth ledge. He held her there, running his wet hands along her sleek, curvaceous legs, hanging in the water in front of him. Continuing his erotic exercise, he watched her eyes as she gently wiped the water drops from his tanned craggy face. "You have beautiful skin, Crissy," he murmured, feeling her tremble under his touch. "But if you don't get out now you're going to end up looking like a wrinkled-up prune." He dodged her kicking foot and hoisted himself next to her. "Time to get out," he ordered, grabbing two towels and giving one to her. "I'm so hungry I could eat a bear. How are you at cooking, woman?"

"Cooking? I thought *you* were going to be the chef this evening, Mr. Prince," she shot back, feeling somewhat distraught that he hadn't kissed her.

"I was thinking more in terms of tossing a salad and snapping some fresh garden beans, and, perhaps if you were up to it, mashing some potatoes."

"I'm a very *good* cook." She bridled, pulling on her short robe and averting her eyes from his scantily clad body.

"And do you cook with love?" he asked her, unceremoniously covering her head with his towel and briskly rubbing her curls.

She came out from under the towel, slightly dizzy from his treatment, and replied giddily, "That, and a lot of herbs and spices."

His hands continued to lean on her proud shoulders. "What else can you do, Crissy? Can you fly?"

"With or without wings?" she responded saucily, turning to leave, but he caught her back against him, holding gently onto her shoulders again.

"Take your pick, honey," he murmured into her neck. She trembled, sighing, and he released her, holding his arms stiffly at his sides.

She continued to walk away, but answered softly, "No." She would let him decide which question she was answering. But she knew she would need nothing more than his loving, strong arms to fly to the moon.

She was absolutely floored when he sped past her in the hall, giving her backside a sound smack as he moved, an impish grin upon his lips. "That's okay, sweetheart. I'll teach you. I've been flying for years!" he informed her as he dodged her snapping towel and strode purposefully into the guest room to change.

"I'll just bet you have, James Robert Prince III," she muttered beneath her breath. "I'll just bet you have!" She almost jumped out of her skin when the door to the room burst open and he asked innocently if she had been talking to him. "No, siree," denied Tulip. "I was jist callin' down the mountain spirits to crimp yore wings a mite."

"But Tulip, that would put us into a tailspin . . . and I don't remember saying anything about using a plane," he crooned, closing the door in her face when she threw her wet towel at him.

She could hear his hearty laughter all the way into the master bedroom, even after she slammed the door and tore off her bikini. She stepped beneath the shower, promising herself he would pay for his teasing . . . in spades!

Five

The meal preparation time was filled with lighthearted banter. James did a lot of running back and forth into the kitchen for salt and pepper, then for the long-handled fork, and then for the warmed serving platter. He constantly interrupted her indoor cooking with cautious suggestions and outright questions about her skill. She took it all with good humor until, in exasperation, she finally threatened to throw her cooking spoon at his head. He retreated backwards, toward the redbird door, and she saw the opportunity to pay him back for his comments. "Your steaks are on fire, James," she informed him sweetly, glancing out the window at the flames rising high above the grill.

He flew out the door to rescue the beef, hopping around like an Indian on the warpath when he burned his finger. She stood at the kitchen window, laughing until the tears ran down her cheeks, but stopped in mid-chuckle when she smelled potatoes. "Oh, drat!" she screamed in frustration. "If I've scorched the potatoes, he'll never let me cook for him again," she cried, suddenly wanting to have the chance to prepare his meals for the rest of her life. She scolded herself for her outlandish daydreams and saved the potatoes just in the knick of time.

Supper was festive. James helped her pile everything onto the serving cart and then pushed it out to the patio, where he arranged the food on the round redwood table. He seated her, then ran back inside to get both of them thick Shetland wool sweaters against the chill of evening. They drank a fine old burgundy with their meal. He insisted they toast to another first in his new home—christening the new barbecue grill and patio table. They laughed again over his impromptu war dance. He ate with the gusto of a growing boy, and when Crissy gently teased him about it, his only response was that he had built up a fierce appetite after all the exercise today.

"Gotta keep my strength up," he said before warning her that she had better eat too so she could ask for a rematch on the courts.

They watched in silent reverence as the sun set in blazing splendor. Crissy never tired of watching the ever-changing purple and crimson spectacle, but tonight she was torn between the sunset and the special look of peace that had stolen over James's face. After their mute vigil, he leaned over to refill her glass, lifting his lightly in a toast. "To sunsets," he murmured. Their eyes caught in smoldering communication.

"And sunrises," she returned on a sigh.

"May they be as spellbinding and mysterious as you," he added, his gaze lowering to her soft mouth. "Ah, Crissy, my mountain gal. Brooklyn was never like this!" he exclaimed warmly, drinking deeply of the sparkling wine, then closing his eyes as he savored the last drop. "Every part of me feels content and full." He softened his tone to a whisper. "Could it be that my status is changing . . . that I'm no longer an outsider?"

She shivered, feeling the caress of his words wrap

around her heart. Was he growing to love the mountains as she did? Or was he trying to knock her off guard again? "At least it's a step in the right direction," she suggested throatily, rising now as she began to feel the dew falling on her skin with the drop in temperature. "Brr, let's clean up here and get our dishes done." They hurried to finish the outdoor chores before summer's last mosquitoes found them.

When she refused to use the dishwasher, James insisted on drying the dishes. He did everything in his power to distract her from her task. He cracked every corny joke he knew, until she was weak with laughter. He came up behind her and plunged his hands into the soapy water with hers, suggesting that it surely would be fun to take a bath with her, but when she threatened him with the last pan, he retreated to finish his job. He wondered aloud if together they might make a good team in the restaurant business. She pointed out to him that she was a teacher and he was a toy-maker. His silken response was, "On second thought, perhaps we should open a preschool . . . and fill it up with a bunch of kids."

James did not allude to the fact that the children could be theirs, but Crissy took the words "we" and "kids" and began to spin her own fairy tale until she blushed with her private thoughts. James teased her mercilessly when he caught the dreamy look on her face. "Where did you go?" he asked softly, pushing an errant curl from her forehead.

"Not very far," she replied mysteriously, drying her hands. "I want to look at the redbird." She switched on the dim light over the table and flipped off the overhead fixture. Then she turned on the outside light and stood to admire the back-lighted art-glass window, each pane glittering brightly. "It *is* lovely."

"Almost as lovely as you, Crissy," he murmured at her ear. She was just about to lean back against him when he moved to the stove and began to pour large cups of steaming coffee, adding a hefty dash of Kahlua to each serving. "Follow me to the den, honey," he invited enticingly. "I'll start a fire."

"Come into my lair," she said, mocking him under her breath. "I'll start a fire . . . and you'll probably use *me* for kindling!" she muttered, darkly, feeling half afraid and half excited at the mere thought.

"What are you mumbling about?" he asked. "Or shouldn't I ask? Maybe you're making some dark, erotic plans for our evening together, huh?" he teased. "Just promise you won't be *too* hard on me, honey. Remember, I've been injured in the line of duty," he cautioned, holding out his blistered little finger.

"Me—be rough on you? Ha! After all I've been through today, I just may curl up on the couch and take a nap," she retorted.

"Now, *that* would be a very *trusting* thing to do, honey." He contradicted his pleasant words with a wickedly raised eyebrow and a dancing gleam in his eyes. He set the cups on the small table by the couch and immediately began to build a roaring fire in the huge fireplace. In moments he was leaning back against the sofa, cup in hand, relaxed and smiling serenely.

"That was fast," she said sleepily, sipping her coffee. "I didn't even hear you strike a match."

"Well, you see, Crissy, there's this little magic button one needs only to press to start the fire. I had a gas pilot light installed," he explained, sheepish now that the secret was out.

"That's cheating," she accused.

"Nope, honey. That's progress!" Then all was still as they watched the dancing flames in the darkened room, feeling the warmth envelop them with a caressing radiance while the Kahlua coffee warmed from within.

Crissy was suddenly too warm, and she placed her cup on the table and pulled the heavy sweater James had lent her over her head, but just as she was going to finish the job, she realized her tulip necklace was caught in one of the loopy threads. "Oh, James," she cried frantically. "My necklace is caught. Help me!"

The sweater was up over her face, her arms trapped inside and pointing straight to the ceiling. James leaned close to her and began the tedious task of unhooking the fine chain. He promised he would be very careful when she cautioned him not to break it. His gentle fingers seemed to take forever, and her arms became tired, so she draped them over the top of her head, complaining, "It's hot inside here. My face is burning up. Hurry!"

"I'm working as quickly as I can, sweetheart," he told her. "Hang on a minute now. It's coming."

"So's Christmas!" she shot back in frustration, but James only chuckled softly at her jab. Neither of them spoke again.

Crissy began to breath claustrophobically inside the knitted trap. Her imagination began to work overtime as she pictured James leaning close to her, enjoying her predicament as he visually explored her defenseless body, covered only by a lacy bra and a thin white T-shirt, along with well-worn jeans. She imagined she could feel his hot breath washing over her skin, which was revealed in the deep scoop neck of her shirt. Or was she only imagining it?

She moaned softly, hoping James would think she was ready to expire inside the woolly sweater, when in reality she could feel her nipples harden and push against her shirt in her self-inflicted arousal. Was he unconscious that his forearms were rubbing softly against her breasts as he tried to release her . . . or was he taking advantage of her again? *"I can't stand it!"* she screamed, but just then James pulled the sweater from her head and comforted her by gently brushing back the damp curly locks from her forehead.

"I'm sorry it took so long, Crissy," he said soothingly. "But I knew you didn't want me to break the chain." Crissy was trying desperately to read the veiled expression in his eyes, not sure if it had been necessary to take so long.

She was as mesmerized by his steady gaze as a

cobra is before its flute-playing master. But she heard no flute, only the gentle rhythmic strumming of a guitar over the stereo hidden somewhere in the den.

Suddenly she believed she could read his thoughts clearly, and though they were alarming to her mind, her body began to respond to the waves of desire that undulated through her limbs, making her weak with longing.

She knew instinctively that he was patiently waiting for her to take the lead. But she worried. Would she be less than he had hoped for? Have a little confidence, she scolded herself, unaware of the visible evidence of her mind-play, which marched across her features.

James was watching her from under hooded lids, fascinated with the expressions flitting over her flushed face. Like a living thing, he felt desire coil inside him. This was the beginning of the game. He wished she would finally stop fighting with herself . . . the tension was driving him crazy!

Finally she gave herself a mental shove and forced herself to smile over at him. "I'm glad you didn't break the chain, James. I would have been terribly upset if my beautiful surprise had been ruined," she murmured. "And I haven't taken the time to think you properly, have I?" she asked in a low, throaty whisper that caused a slight shudder to run along James's relaxed arm, lying along the back of the sofa. She felt the tremor when she ran her hand lightly from his wrist to his cheek. Taking a deep breath, she leaned forward and placed a warm kiss upon his parted lips. She almost screamed in frustration when she realized he was not going to participate any further than supplying his mouth as her target; he was *not* going to pull her against him in a wild embrace.

He might have thought he was making her suffer, but in truth, he was, by remaining immobile and completely still, giving her whirling mind and aroused body more fuel than she thought she might be able to cope with. I'll melt you, you great iceberg, she swore silently. This is just another one of your tricks!

And in that same moment, James realized he had found the tactic that would bring her to him. Competition! He couldn't have her unless he was strong enough to keep refusing her.

Slowly she pushed away from his chest and whispered in her best *femme fatale* voice, "Thank you . . . for the necklace *and* the kiss."

He smiled warmly. "My pleasure, honey." But he sat still, his eyes filled with challenge. He was waiting for her next move . . . if, in fact, there would be one, because he was determined to control himself tonight. She was going to come to him! But, dammit, she looked so lovely and desirable here by the fire, he thought feverishly.

"Aren't you warm with that sweater on, James?" she asked softly, slipping her fingers tentatively along the edge at his hips. "Let me help you take it off," she cajoled, taking hold of the bottom edge with both hands as he sat up to help her. He lifted his arms above his head, and she had to rise on her knees on the sofa in order to pull it off. She took her own sweet time about it, moving her palms up over his wide, muscled chest, then reaching around to his back to lift the sweater, her breasts barely grazing the front of his torso. When she finally finished this task, she could feel his ragged breath surging against her, but she suspected he was perhaps even more bullheaded than she. He was like a great stone-faced mountain, she fumed silently, unmindful that she might be falling into her own trap.

"Now, isn't that better?" she crooned. "I'll bet you feel much cooler now, don't you?"

"Much!" he informed her stoically. "Thank you for *all* your help."

"My pleasure, James," she answered, frazzled now, but continuing her attack on his senses with long sensual strokes of her hands on his bare arms and around his open collar. "You still feel warm to me," she observed. "That's a real blaze we've got going," she told him, catching the grin that was twitching at the corners of his thick moustache. "I'm afraid you're going to become overheated." She plunged ahead, beginning now to unbutton the front of his shirt with jerky, nervous motions. When she pulled the tails of his shirt unceremoniously from his belted jeans, he could not control the gasp that shot from his lips. She, however, ignored his reaction, fighting for control herself. He was driving her crazy!

With gentle massaging circles she rubbed both hands over his chest, reveling in the feel of his hair-roughened flesh, aware of the throbbing beat of his heart, and more than a little afraid of his reaction as she finally settled her fingertips over his hard, flat nipples. She could almost hear the restraints snapping. She was beyond caring now, caught, too, but determined more than ever to force him to take control.

She smiled sweetly into his smoldering eyes, murmuring in a low, vibrant whisper, "Give up, James!"

He shook his head slowly. "No way, baby. This is kid's stuff!"

She couldn't believe her ears, but her eyes snapped, telling him he was going to eat those words. His only reply was a challenging grin.

She slowly dropped her head to blow her hot breath across his bare torso and place tiny butterfly kisses over the wide expanse of his chest. Not lifting her lips, she guided her head in a torturous path up to his ear, then down, to pause at the telling pulse beating in his throat, and then zeroing in, crossing over the line of good sense, to his nipples, where she alternated with lips and tongue as she sucked at each tip. She had never been so brazen, even with her young husband, but she just *had* to bring James down. It was a matter of principle now!

She could not suppress a wicked snicker when she felt his hands fluttering like untamed birds along her sides. But when he heard her laugh of triumph, he thrust his untrustworthy hands deep into the pockets of his jeans and grimly refused to surrender. By God, he was going to win if it killed him!

Exasperated, she pulled away from him and knelt at his side, a vexed angel wondering what else she could do. He was so experienced. He probably knew every way there was to arouse and become aroused.

"Have you run out of ideas?" he prodded. "If so, I'll be glad to take over . . . that is, when you ask me . . . nicely." That silky request was for unconditional surrender, she realized in alarm. Oh, why did he have to be so darned obstinate? Think, brain!

A sudden idea came to mind, and she leaned over and planted a quick kiss on his unsuspecting lips. "Don't go away, James. I'll be right back." She flew from the room back to the kitchen, where she poured a generous portion of high-proof, expensive brandy into a small snifter. She paused only to remove her wisp of a bra, tossing it carelessly onto the counter, and then put her T-shirt on again. All the while she was lecturing herself.

Okay, you started this. Just remember that. You're not a little girl, you're a woman . . . and you have to win this one! She took a deep breath and walked in graceful serenity back to the den.

She found him right where she had left him. "Why, James, I don't think you moved a muscle." He admitted there was no place else he'd rather be, but she caught the sudden blaze in his blue eyes when they fastened hungrily upon her unfettered breasts. Their aroused tips made prominent points in her tight T-shirt. Even in the firelight the rosy circles were evident through the thin white fabric.

Get hold of yourself, man, James cautioned his protesting body. She's going to win if you don't watch yourself. His male ego took over then. I can take anything . . . even if she fights dirty! He took a deep breath. "You're very beautiful," he complimented her smoothly. "But you're still no competition for me, baby. This is the big time!"

Fighting mad now, she put the snifter next to their empty cups and settled herself beside his relaxed form.

Silently she pushed his shirt off his strong, wide shoulders and tossed it carelessly behind the couch. Then she kicked off her shoes and invited him to do the same. She reached for the brandy with one hand and, without speaking, gently shoved against his bare chest, playfully fingering the hair as she pushed him into a half-reclining position. His gaze narrowed suspiciously, and he wondered if she would be foolish enough to throw the liquor in his face.

"Now, this is brandy," she instructed him in a firm voice, holding the glass up to the light. "Its alcoholic content is very high; therefore, it has a cooling effect, thanks to the fact that it evaporates quickly when applied to the skin," she theorized confidently, not really knowing what the hell she was talking about. She lifted the snifter and sipped the brandy, then offered the glass to his lips, tipping it up so he would have to take a large mouthful.

"*Now* for the treatment," she continued mysteriously. Her voice broke at the audacity of her intended action. She dipped her fingers into the liquid and began to rub it over his chest. Then she leaned forward. Her heart almost leaped from her chest with her rising excitement when she began to lick the brandy from his skin, pushing against him when he seemed incapable of suppressing his moan of pleasure.

"Lie down, James," she ordered softly. "I'm losing it," she explained, meaning that the brandy was running down his skin too quickly.

You're losing it? he thought. I'm damn near lost! he reminded himself, grimly fighting with his last ounce of strength to keep from throwing her down on the rug. To Crissy, he observed in goading nonchalance, "You're going to have to do better than that. I'm not even breathing hard."

She felt like slapping the bored grin from his face, but she continued. The brandy burned her lips, while her lips burned his skin. She knew she couldn't stand much more of this herself, and was almost at the point of begging him to make love to her. Suddenly a good idea came to her. She pulled herself away from his body, fully aware of his need, whether he admitted it or not, and she said excitedly, "Sit up, James."

He did as she asked, but grumbled, "I wish you'd make up your mind, honey."

"Well, 'honey,' you'll have to excuse my wandering ways. This is very new to me," she told him lightly, too engrossed in her next attack on his senses to be upset by his gentle scolding. "Come on, turn around," she insisted.

"If you're tired and bored, James, maybe a back rub will relax you." She clucked maternally. "Just close your eyes." Once he did, she began to gently massage his tight neck, running her fingers up into his thick hair, then down along his spine. She continued this exercise until she thought *she* would scream. When she couldn't stand it another instant, she rubbed with one hand while she wiggled out of her T-shirt, then exchanged hands to finish the job, dropping the shirt on the floor on top of his.

"Now, sit very still, James. I think *this is going to do it*," she declared softly, blowing her hot breath over his skin just before she leaned forward to put her arms around his body and rub her thrusting bare breasts over his back in burning circles of delight. Her fingers found his flat nipples and held him tightly while she flicked gently over the hard edge with her rounded nails.

Instantly James catapulted off the sofa as if the cushions had suddenly exploded. "Lift-off!" Crissy announced smugly beneath her breath, and her delight knew no bounds as he rocketed away from her arms.

In one long stride he was at the chest-high wooden mantel, leaning heavily against it and gasping for breath as he fought against the combustible attraction of her body. He rested his head on his white-knuckled hands. "Thank you very much for the back rub," he ground out through a clenched jaw. He continued to keep his back turned away from Crissy, blocking the heat and light from the blazing logs.

An elfin grin pulled at the corners of Crissy's full mouth. That had done it. She had won! She still sat on her legs, torso straight and nude, her outstretched hands slowly settling upon the back of the sofa.

For some reason, she felt no need to cover herself. Dared she speak . . . even softly? she wondered, knowing with a woman's instinct that he was using the last reserves of his superhuman control. She watched in fascination as he continued to fight. His shoulders rounded in the effort, as if he were going down for the count. The smile of satisfaction at a job well done spread over her serene face, and she sighed theatrically, moving in for the kill. "James?" she goaded in a throaty whisper, "you don't seem very relaxed to me."

"Well, what the hell did you expect?" he bellowed like a wounded bull elephant, spinning around to face her. But the rest of his tirade died in his throat when he beheld her nude beauty, her soft, proud breasts erect and beckoning to him. He literally fell against the mantel, the thud of his overwhelmed body drowned out by his exclamation. "Oh . . . my . . . God!" He groaned, his voice filled with desire and misery. He staggered to the side, still hanging on to the mantel, feeling himself melt from the combination of outer and inner heat. He knew his jeans were about to ignite, and the fire from the logs was nothing compared to his own. He swallowed noisily, bringing the satisfied smile to Crissy's lips again.

He knew he had to speak, he had to fight . . . but the will had left him when he looked at her—warm and enticingly beautiful in the golden light of the flickering firelight.

Finally he found his raspy voice, but his tongue felt thick. "You've pushed me to the limit, you little vamp," he accused harshly. "But as you can plainly see, I've kept my vow not to touch you. You *haven't* won! And your little exercise in trying to make me take advantage of you has failed. I'm stronger than you . . . but I'm sure you enjoyed yourself immensely!"

He prayed that the Tulip in her would have a flip comeback so he could rechannel his turbulent emotions. Never had he found himself in such a vulnerable position. He always kept the upper hand in any situation. Always, in the past, he had been able to maintain control. But with Crissy, beautiful, relaxed woman that she was, sitting just a step away from him in all her feminine glory, he could not trust himself. He shook his head silently, realizing he had finally met his match!

Fight, dammit, woman. Fight! he entreated with smoldering eyes and grim features, which veiled the pain of his repressed passion. He hadn't ached like this for sexual release since he was a boy experiencing his first erotic urges. But with Crissy, he felt so much more. She did not speak, just continued to watch him with her sensual, dark eyes. Feeling close to the breaking point, he hissed sarcastically, "Well . . . you did enjoy yourself, didn't you?" The ache had risen into his throat now, so that it actually hurt to speak.

He almost self-destructed when Crissy sighed and stretched languidly, bringing her arm down behind the sofa to pick up his discarded shirt. Her breasts were so taut and inviting; her skin glowed with warmth and reflected light. He felt his fingernails dig into the mantel, sure his prints would remain forever in the hard, hand-hewn wood, and he turned his back on her beauty, staring down into the fire, still seeing her body in his mind.

Quietly Crissy slipped the shirt over her nude torso, not bothering to button it, just leaving it open down the front, still revealing a wide strip of tanned flesh but modestly covering her bare breasts. Soundlessly she got up from the soft couch and took steps that brought her mere inches from his stiff, defiant form. James jerked his head up, startled, when he heard her voice so near.

"I did enjoy myself," she assured him in a warm,

gentle voice, "but I think I might enjoy myself more . . . if you participated," she suggested. Tentatively she placed her fingertips on his shoulders, and took great pleasure in the heat of his body. He turned around, feeling her tender touch scorch his sensitized skin as her hands trailed around him.

"Is that an invitation?" he pushed on with determination. But he smiled triumphantly, his hot breath warming her upraised face. He still had enough control to hold his hands at his sides, although he wanted to crush her to him. Unyielding, he had to make her accede to his terms. "Are you now willing to give me your heart and soul . . . *and* your body? I told you I'd settle for nothing less, Crissy," he reminded her, a seductive quality shading his words. "You can't hold *anything* back."

She continued to stroke his bare flesh, fire flowing from her touch, burning pathways of desire across his chest. She looked deeply into his shadowed eyes. "You can have all of me . . . for a little while. But there is one provision to my surrender, James." He raised a quizzical eyebrow. "I'll accept nothing less from you," she said with determination. "I want all of *you*, with nothing held back . . . at least for a little while," she cautioned. "Agreed?"

James felt the last of his resistance evaporate like steam under the intense heat of her steady, beckoning eyes. Silently he nodded, then murmured, "Agreed! But, Crissy, I may not be able to return all of you, sweetheart. I may have to keep just a little part of you. Call it a remembrance."

"Like the red silk scarf," she stated with understanding. He nodded again, watching her reaction to his words, wondering if she would fight his condition, but it was she who threw James completely off-balance with her reply. "And I think *you* may find, dearest James, that you will not remain completely untouched." Her lips curved into a sweet, feminine smile, beguiling his senses, releasing his final control. Crissy was operating on instinct alone now; she had never before become so involved with a man—not even her husband, because they had been so young, both so inexperienced, playing at love.

James's and Crissy's gazes locked. He reached out to touch her hand, nestled in the thick hair of his chest. He encircled her fingers and, still gazing openly into her wide, smoky eyes, he brought them to his warm lips, kissing each fingertip. Erotically he licked at her sensitized skin, finally thrusting her index finger into his mouth and slowly sucking at it while she rubbed it against his tongue and along his white, straight teeth.

"You're mine, Crissy," he whispered in a voice throbbing with certainty. "My own enticing witch. You're mine," he repeated, sweeping her up into his arms and striding toward the master bedroom. She wrapped her arms around his neck, surrendering, and pulled herself closer into his strong embrace, feeling his desire for her in his touch. Inside the dark room, he paused to turn the switch on a small lamp on the dresser, which shimmered softly. Then he pulled the drapes closed and she knew they were shut off from the rest of the world. This time was theirs alone.

Slowly he released her legs, to let her body slide to a standing position before him. His hands were warm and caressing against her back as he spoke one last time. "No reservations, Crissy. Nothing held back, sweetheart. Agreed?"

"If you agree to the same terms, James," she answered stubbornly, still determined to get the same commitment from him.

His nod was answered with hers, each sighing in complete surrender to the moment. The room was lighted just enough to show their features and aroused forms in shadowed textures. James tenderly pushed his shirt from her shoulders, and she felt its softness fall from her arms to her bare feet. With an exquisite touch he traced her shoulders, her collarbone, the high, agitated rise of her breasts, all the while that his eyes drank in her glowing beauty.

Her fingers caught at the belt loops on the sides of his jeans; she felt she had to hold onto something or she would collapse from the tension he was creating. He raised his hungry gaze to her face, locking eyes with her wide, passionate, almost black ones. Then he watched silently when the pupils enlarged and darkened even further as he masterfully caressed her breasts, rubbing his thumbs across her hard nipples, then gently pinching in a touch of pleasure-pain. Her breathing became shallow and fast with his experienced touch. She licked her lips unselfconsciously, moving along on an age-old path known to all women since the beginning of time.

Light-headed, Crissy swayed against his hands, and he dropped them to her narrow waist, pulling her against his chest with a light touch, moving her slowly back and forth across his skin. He felt his body surge with a desire he could see mirrored on her passionate face. "How I've longed to feel you." He groaned as if in pain. She could not speak, but stretched her arms around his back to pull him closer. And when she raised her lips to his, the blue lightning of the kiss set them on fire. His tongue was a thrusting torment to her senses, and she rose to meet his demand with one of her own, each giving and receiving the full measure of the kiss.

He continued to shower her skin with tantalizing, hot, moist kisses, marking a pathway to her throbbing breasts. When he fastened his mouth around a hard bud, she pushed against his touch, trying to fill him with herself. He moaned with the pleasure she gave by her movement, and he fell to his knees, expertly removing her jeans and undies. In moments she stood before him, straight and proud, taking satisfaction in his visually devouring exploration of her firm, tanned body. "You're exquisite, Crissy," he murmured, unable to stop his searing touch along her limbs.

Balking charmingly at this one-sided game, she quickly divested James of his jeans and briefs, then stood back for a moment to gaze hungrily at his nude body, dwelling at leisure on the source of his manhood, shivering in anticipation when she was tempted to touch him. "And *you* are magnificent," she crooned throatily, finally overcoming the last of vestiges of shyness to stroke him with her open palm.

"Oh, Crissy!" He chuckled erotically, moving her gently to the bed a moment after he tossed back the covers. "I knew you would be passionate, my darling witch . . . but I never imagined how wanton you might be." When she stiffened in his arms, he hurriedly implored, "Don't stop, baby. You're exactly what I want . . . what I need. Don't ever put that wall up again," he ordered, effectively cutting off any response with his parted lips.

The kiss went on and on. She could feel their bodies melting in rising fire. They kissed until Crissy felt she had no more breath in her, and she fell to the bed. She felt herself slipping and sliding over the smooth sheets. She opened her eyes to look, and was surprised to see that she was lying on red satin sheets. She looked up at James, who was still standing beside the bed, wearing nothing more than a satisfied grin. "James, red satin sheets?"

"I find that red is becoming my favorite color . . . too," he answered agreeably, watching her as she stretched with feline grace upon the sheets. "Rule number one," he recited drolly. "If you're determined to win, then prepare for the victory." She nodded her understanding, and his eyes took on a darker, burning hue when she beckoned him to her side. "Crissy, you look like soft whipped cream on top of fresh, succulent strawberries," he said adoringly, running his fingers up along her smooth legs.

"You must be hungry," she purred, stretching lazily. "You're talking about food again."

"I am hungry . . . for you." He growled, kissing her

hard. His hands never stopped their fiery exploration, nor did hers. Each of them found and ignited the other's pleasure points. Garbled words of endearment and encouragement drove them to the place where minds surrendered to bodies.

Breathless with anticipation, Crissy knew it was time, and she parted her legs willingly beneath his insistent thigh. A moment before he entered her secret warmth, he stopped, hovering above her, and his smoky, aroused eyes sought hers. His breathing was ragged, his body tense and rigid. "*All* of you, Crissy. Remember that," he ordered gruffly.

She smiled sensuously and murmured her reply. "All of *you*, James." Then she arched her hips to his throbbing loins, beginning the journey to utopia. Her answer released a torrent of energy in James. There was no gentleness after the first few thrusts. Once he had determined that he wasn't hurting her, he surrendered everything to the moment and plunged against her, into her, with a surging power that rocked Crissy to her soul.

His abandoned lovemaking was beyond her limited experience. His body was awakening passions that until this moment, had been unknown to her. It seemed the whole room was galloping to their erotic cadence, and Crissy grasped his thrusting flesh with her arms and legs, bringing all her strength into the movement, feeling her body hold his everywhere. She was reaching, clawing, for the ecstasy she hoped would come, and when it arrived, she cried out in total release, her heat coiling and convulsing around him. An instant later, his perspiration-soaked body collapsed against her writhing, wave-tossed form. Then all was still, save the gasping breath of them both, as they rode the climactic storm to its conclusion.

"So sweet . . . so much," he whispered in praise, stroking the moist ringlets off her forehead.

"Yes," was all Crissy could reply, still feeling the splendor of their lovemaking as she held him in her arms.

He continued to stroke her hair, tracing her features, soothing her warm skin. "It's been a long time for you, hasn't it, darling?" It was more an observation than a question.

"Since my husband," she answered softly, knowing in her heart that this time had actually been her first time as a full-grown mature woman. "I told you I never had difficulty saying no . . . before you, James," she added shyly. Then she laughed self-consciously. "And you knew if you stayed away from me, yet let me know how much you wanted me, I'd feel compelled to try to make you fail, didn't you? I like to win too much, I think." She sighed, running her nails along his embracing arm.

He chuckled at her comment. "I think, in this case, we're *both* winners, Crissy. It was good for you, sweetheart, wasn't it? I tried to be gentle—at least, at first—but I couldn't. Not when I'd promised to hold nothing back. Not when I could feel you, so completely involved." He paused. "*Was* it good for you, honey?"

Crissy was finally coming down from the heights of her passion, and the little imp of her teasing personality rose to answer his question. "Compared to what, mister?" Tulip chortled. "Land's sake! I'm jist a backwoods country gal. I ain't an experienced city-slicker like yo'all."

With the quickness of a panther, he rolled on top of her wiggling, giggling body, pinning her to the soft mattress. "Go away, Tulip," he commanded. "It's time Crissy had a wider field of experience for valid comparison."

She was shocked into complete submission by his next actions, which were so erotic and abandoned that she could only lay beneath him, wide-eyed and confused by the feelings he called up from her trembling body. "You think you gave me everything the first time, little innocent?" he asked, grinning mischievously as he worked miracles upon her flesh. "Now you're going to get a lesson in just how much you have to give! You don't have any idea of the passion your beautiful body has concealed all these years. But, baby"—he spoke into her ear, his hot breath and words making her shudder with his threat—"I'm just the man to give you some food for thought. Now, follow my lead, sweetheart. I believe in *learning by doing*!" He emphasized the last words, beginning to move his head and his limbs in the most suggestive manner. His knowing hands stroked her, and were followed by his hot, wet mouth and tongue. She could feel the heat rise in her loins as he traced the length of her body. Moving to her flat belly, he sucked her soft skin, pausing only to shout triumphantly, "Honey, I'm fixin' to send you higher than a kite, my gorgeous, inexperienced mountain gal!"

She giggled seductively, raking her bare feet along his tensed, muscular legs, feeling her toes rub against his hairy skin. "Don't bet on it, feller," she dared, giggling again. But just then, he threw her legs apart and lowered his mouth to her body, holding her hips in an iron vise as he plundered her heat. She groaned in surprise and shock and tried to dig her heels into the bed to push herself away from him. Her actions only gave him greater access; he was following her movements with distressing accuracy. *"James!"* she cried out, half in excitement and half in fear. "I can't breathe," she gasped.

For just an instant, he raised his head and looked darkly into her wild eyes. There was a savage-sweet smile upon his wide, firm lips. His moustache curved upward with his devilish grin. "Have you ever swooned, Crissy?" he asked teasingly.

"Only for Magnum," she shot back, trying desperately to regain her composure.

"Does a man with a moustache send you, honey?" he teased right back. Not waiting for any retort she might offer, he ran his mouth across her breasts and down along the center of her trembling belly, chuckling when he felt her uninhibited response. "Just close your eyes and imagine a warm, woolly caterpillar is exploring your many charms, Crissy," he suggested, continuing his tickling, erotic searching of her body. "Just remember, he'll always go for the heat . . . he wants to be where it's hot . . . and, baby, I think he's just found the right spot!" he enthused, moving his mouth against her again.

James's lesson in love went on nonstop until Crissy was crying out in ecstasy. He was driving her to the edge of her desire, and she surrendered to his thrilling touch, feeling the heat push her beyond her control. She shuddered and trembled in his arms, her eyes closed to the world, reveling in the erotic sensations he had summoned with his words and touch. She had moved to another plane of existence, unaware that James lay on his side, watching every twitch and cherishing every sigh and choked cry of her release.

His touch had lightened to that of butterfly wings as he continued for her pleasure, but when she seemed to rouse from her trancelike state, he silently rolled her over on her stomach, totally conscious of the fact that she was still in the throes of her heightened response. He straddled her legs and began to massage and knead her flesh, running his fingertips temptingly along her ribs and the sides of her crushed breasts. His lips followed suit, until every inch of her exposed skin had been covered with his kisses and exciting touch. She could feel the intensity begin to rise again to a new level when he massaged and stroked the back of her thighs, running his fingers deeply between them. She moaned again, rising up on her hands and knees to come to him, but instead, he pulled her back against his kneeling body and continued to tantalize her senses by firmly touching her breasts and nipples and inner core. She could not reach him, but she could feel him surge against her rounded, tense bottom.

"James," she pleaded, "please . . . *please!*" She dug her nails into his legs and arms, unable to reach his torso. "I can't take any more."

He rolled away from her and lay back against the

pillows, cushioning his head with his arms, smiling happily at her heartfelt complaint. "Then, little darlin', it's my turn, mmm?" He watched closely as Crissy's eyes devoured his lean, supple form.

"You're not even breathing hard!" she gasped with sudden understanding, her heart hammering away in double time.

His gaze smoldered, and challenging lights sparkled in his eyes. "Maybe you should try to *make* me," he suggested. "But I warn you, I'm in very good condition."

"And hard as nails," she observed, suggestively glancing down at his aroused manhood. Then, she spoke no more, nor did she respond to his sensually chuckled retort.

"If I had a ham-mer!" he sang merrily, but Crissy's thoughts answered challengingly. I'll hammer you, she decided, taking up his dare, determined to make him surrender to her.

She was still breathing heavily when she started her assault on his tanned body. The heat of her breath seemed to announce an end to the teasing and the beginning of an intense foreplay that brought James into the vortex of her circle of desire. "Do you like this, James?" she crooned, moving over him. "And this . . . and this?" His silent response came directly from his body when he began to squirm under her firm, massaging touch. He muttered darkly beneath his breath. Crissy only caught a word or two of his suggestive expletive. She chuckled, moving her hot attack to his loins. "James!" she scolded gently. "You must be losing control. I've never heard such language."

She realized at once that she should not have pushed him quite so far, because his hands came from beneath his rocking head and joined the fight, adding fuel to the fire when his fingers plunged along her crouched body. This was more than she could handle! She wanted to argue that he wasn't playing fair, but she had come too far . . . her mind had relinquished its hold on her rapier tongue and biting teeth. He groaned, moving to meet her murmur of pleasure. She could feel the tension coil inside her, and she threw her leg over his writhing limbs. "Give up!" she ordered, her voice a quivering hiss.

"Never!" he proclaimed. "Make me!" And she lowered herself onto him with a force that took his breath away. He grabbed her hard bottom, convulsed and contracting with her will to ride him like a stallion. He was effectively trapped inside her now, and he watched, like one in an erotic dream, all the contortions of her face as she rose and fell against him in an anguished rhapsody of love. On and on she drove him, until he thought he would break in two or shatter her into a million pieces. He could stand no more, and he flung her to the bed and regained control . . . crying out to her . . . driving her to the wildest reaches of rapture.

In the throes of this battle for supremacy, James had not counted on her defiant will to win. He was losing control, unable to stop himself as he plunged into her hot, moist body. He shuddered and fell, broken, gasping in his release. But in the next moment he was brought to a sudden awareness of a pulsating sensation, when he felt her climactic, grasping upheaval. She clung to him, and he held her with the strength of ten men, feeling victorious and beaten in the same throbbing moment.

After they had both caught their breaths, and he had rolled to her side, she smiled up into his flushed face, pulling gently at his moustache, which he seemed incapable even of twitching back at her. "Have you nothing to say?" she asked proudly.

"All I can say . . . all I can wheeze . . . is: '*Uncle!*' " he choked out.

"Is that all?" she replied, pushing for a compliment, unmindful of how she might sound.

"How about, 'I . . . am . . . driven!' " he sang in an exhausted voice.

She laughed softly, kissing his relaxed lips and

getting little response because he was completely spent. "I think that commercial might have been written for us both." It seemed a mighty effort for James to nod his agreement.

He lay beside her, holding her in his loose embrace, still breathing unevenly, as he sighed with wonder at her wild response. And he knew then that he could live a lifetime with this woman and never get his fill. He relived her power to arouse his senses and her strength to bend his will to hers. There had been one point when he had truly tried to fight off her sensual advances, wanting her to beg for fulfillment. But the battle had been useless, so ardent had she been in overcoming his feebly acted disinterest. She had set his body afire with a blaze that even he, with all his years of experience, had never known. She was a giving creature of pleasure, he decided, and with one lesson in love she had become a marvel of inventiveness, pushing aside her reserves of shyness and almost destroying him with her lusty response. Yes, he had met his match, he thought, kissing her moist ringlets in total surrender.

She lay beside him, feeling satiated and complete. A part of her was awed by what she had just done. Another part of her was terribly proud of her willful behavior. She'd given as good as she'd gotten, she thought happily. Never had she experienced such fulfillment. She was a sexual being. He had made her aware of herself . . . and she could spend the rest of her life learning from him. She kissed his warm chest softly, without passion, for she had no more to give at the moment.

They lay there in each other's arms, unaware that both entertained the same thought: I could love this loving creature. And the wonder of each one's feelings pulled them together into a warm embrace.

They drifted into a deep, dreamless sleep for almost two hours. Then Crissy awakened and told James she had to leave.

Six

It was after 2:00 in the morning when Crissy arrived back at her little cottage in the woods. She was tired, but also very happy. After what they had just shared, James *must* have deep feelings for her. "Oh, please, let him fall in love with me," she prayed. "I need his love . . . so much."

She smiled when she recalled his insistent pleading that she stay the night. "I want to keep sleeping with you in my arms. I want to wake up the same way, Crissy," he had said as they lay together. But she had been adamant in her refusal, though she wanted their time to go on forever. She had explained that she couldn't leave her car parked in the restaurant lot all night, and reminded him that she was a working girl and had a job to do in the morning.

He had tried to kiss her back into submission then, but she had wiggled free, dressing quickly and suggesting that he might want to cover himself if he was going to drive her to her car. "You don't want to shock some innocent night critter, do you?" she had teased. He had pulled on his jeans and walked outside with her arm in arm, whispering into her receptive ear that he wouldn't mind shocking a few night critters if he could have his way with one particularly alluring feminine creature!

She touched her fingertips to her mouth, feeling the heat of his last kiss. She trembled with desire, knowing she had never been kissed with such intensity by any man.

"Whew!" she whistled softly, pressing the button that would rewind her phone-answering device. She fell across the bed and reached over to her nightstand to pick up pen and note pad in case she needed to jot down a number or a message.

"Five two one two," she heard herself saying at the beginning of the tape. "Please leave your message at the sound of the tone and your party will return your call as soon as possible." She never stated her name, because it was impossible to tell who would be calling, or who the caller might want—Crissy or Belle.

"Crissy, this is Katie," said the first caller. "I have some information for you. Very important. Call back at once. I don't care if you do wake me up. I love you."

Crissy frowned in concentration, jotting Katie's name on her paper. I wonder what she wants. Maybe another job.

"Belle, this is Jack Hanley," stated the next voice. "We've got a rush commercial here, set for recording at eleven tomorrow morning. This is an emergency, Belle. I'm counting on you, sweetheart. I need you!" said the suggestive voice, and Crissy smiled knowingly at the tone. She had dated Jack for several months now, whenever she was called to St. Louis to do a commercial with his company. "Your tickets are waiting for you at the Springfield airport. The plane leaves at 6:00 A.M. sharp. Don't fail me, Belle. I'll pick you up when you get in. See ya, gorgeous lady." And she made another scrawl on her note pad.

She turned off the machine; there were no more

calls. But she did not pick up the phone to call Katie just then. She relaxed against the bed pillows, silently comparing her friend Jack with James. Both were very successful. Both were extremely attractive and well educated. She enjoyed each man's company, as well as his kisses. But then she trembled again, feeling James's touch upon her flushed body, knowing she had not experienced Jack's brand of lovemaking only because she'd never felt that involved with him. And there the comparison died. After all these months, she still considered Jack a good friend, although he had continued to encourage her to think about him in terms of becoming an ardent lover.

Crissy sat up and reached for the phone, dialing quickly and preparing herself for a long wait until she could break into the fanciful dreamworld of her dear friend Katie. She was surprised when, on the second ring, Katie's breathless voice came on the line.

"Crissy, is that you?" Katie said in a rush. Crissy laughingly acknowledged her question, asking if she had been sitting up all night waiting for her. "Well, I have to admit I did have a thing or two to tell you." Not waiting for any response, Katie plunged on. "I've been digging into James Robert Prince III's background, and apparently he disappointed a lot of women when he left New York." Crissy's heart began to contract in pain, not wanting to hear what her friend had to say. "He was just very, very popular with the ladies but, according to the rumors, never was serious about any one woman."

Fears and doubts began slowly building inside Crissy. If not one woman in New York could have held James . . .

"So my advice to you," Katie went on, "is to take it real slow and casual. From everything I've heard he's a dangerous man to get attached to."

Crissy leaned her forehead on one hand. What had she gotten herself into? "I think your advice comes a little too late, Katie."

"Oh, no, Crissy! What happened?"

"I've just come from his home, Katie. I'm falling in love with him . . . and I gave him everything."

"Everything?"

"Everything," Crissy admitted frankly, knowing her words would go no farther than the ear of her trusted friend. "What should I do?"

Katie took a deep breath. Realistically she pointed out, "As I see it, you have two choices. You can fight for him . . . or you can run like hell!"

"They may be one and the same," Crissy commented wryly. "He has a competitive streak a mile wide."

"Then do both!" Katie shot back. "Damn, girl, if he's worth your love, he's worth the fight, right?" she asked. "Right?"

"I don't know if I can fight him, Katie. He really gets to me," Crissy answered dejectedly.

"Men like that are the only kind worth going after, honey," retorted her friend with conviction. "I should be so lucky to have that kind of man all hot and bothered over me."

Crissy blushed, and scolded Katie for her outrageous comment, but her friend was insistent. "I mean it, Crissy. You've got what it takes. You're going to perform for the Crown Prince," she teased, trying to get Crissy into a better frame of mind. "What the hell do you think you went to college for?"

"Not to get a man," Crissy yelled, rising to Katie's challenging words as only one friend could do with another.

"You learned to act, silly goose," Katie responded. "So act!"

"Do you think I should try Garbo or Fontaine?" she countered sarcastically.

"That's the spirit, honey," cheered Katie, giggling now that Crissy was primed to take up the challenge. She knew her friend rather well, she thought smugly. "Just give him a run for his money, babe. It'll drive him crazy!"

"He's crazy as a fox already, Katie," she declared spiritedly. "But I promise you I won't draw him any road map. And maybe, just maybe, I can keep him interested," she said musingly, already conjuring the wished-for final chapter to her impending mysterious adventure. "Gotta fly, honey . . . to St. Louis," she told her friend. "Thanks for the pep talk. I may need you to help me pick up the pieces if I don't win the war," she cautioned, only partly in jest.

"He won't know what hit him," Katie assured her. "I only wish I could be there to see the play unfold. Good luck," she added seriously.

"I'm going to need it."

"You don't have to have luck, Crissy," her friend whispered fondly. "You've got love on your side. Keep me posted. Love you." And she was gone.

Quietly Crissy replaced the receiver in its cradle, pondering Katie's parting words. "Do I really have love on my side?" she wondered aloud. "Is it possible James is beginning to love me?" She couldn't unravel all the pieces. Not now. She had a job to do, and would not allow her mind to dwell upon her growing deep feelings for him. But she did not move. She continued to sit on the edge of the bed, lost in thought. When the telephone rang, she started, as the jangle brought her back to the present. She reached for the phone in exasperation, sure it was Jack calling to change the work plans.

"Five two one two," she answered, curtly, using her real voice. She clutched her throat with a trembling hand when James's voice came booming over the line.

"I've been trying to reach you for an hour, Crissy," he informed her in a worried voice. "Are you all right?"

She swallowed hard, trying to still the nervous tremors rising in her chest. "Yes, I'm all right, James," she responded softly.

"Your phone has been busy. Who in the world were you talking to at this hour?" he asked, past the point in his worry about her well being to remember it was none of his business.

Crissy realized his lack of good manners spoke more of his concern for her than of his possessiveness. But certainly she couldn't tell him the truth . . . that she had been speaking with Katie about him! She searched her mind for an alternative satisfactory response. "I was talking to my granny," she said.

"At two-thirty in the morning?" he croaked in disbelief. "Is she ill?" he added on a softer note.

"No, Granny is just fine," she replied. "Only lonely."

"I know the feeling," he retorted, and Crissy's heart skipped a beat.

"She's been trying to get me all day," Crissy explained, baldly lying. "She said she woke up and thought of me, so she tried to call one more time. She just wanted to visit, James."

"What did you talk about?" James asked, and Crissy smiled at his sly attempt to find out how she herself was feeling about their time together.

She relaxed against her propped-up pillows and cradled the phone to her ear. "Oh, this and that," she teased, sharing an intimate chuckle with him. He wanted to know what Granny had thought about their spending the day together. "She thought it was a mite long to be called a picnic," she replied, scurrying through her mind to find just the right words for what she was about to say. "And she gave me a warning!"

"What?" he squawked, his voice rising in agitation. "She doesn't even know me!"

Crissy continued to speak very softly, intimately. "Granny told me I'd better watch my step because, from what she could tell, it sounded as if I was smitten with you." There! She had said it just right, she thought. The hook had been baited, but would he bite? She lay on her bed, afraid to breathe, but at his reply, her heart almost burst with joy.

"Sounds as if your wise Granny might have been giving us *both* good advice, huh?" he whispered sensuously. "I don't exactly know what to call what I'm feeling for you, honey, but 'smitten' seems very appropriate at the moment. I can't stop thinking about you . . . and what we shared tonight. I want you, baby . . . all the time and in every way." He groaned. "Crissy, my sophisticated mountain gal, I'm never going to be the same again."

She put her hand over the receiver a moment before the gasp of joy escaped from her lips. She moaned, tightly shutting her eyes against the hot tears streaming unchecked down her cheeks. He *did* care for her. "Oh, James," she whispered, her hand still muffling the phone. She heard his voice breaking through her silence.

"Crissy? Crissy, have we been cut off? Damn!" he muttered. "Crissy?"

She pulled herself together, determined not to reveal to him her true feelings of happiness. "Mmmm? James, what did you say? I'm so sleepy that I must have dozed off." Her body was as filled with her desire for him as it had been earlier.

He chuckled throatily, picturing her gorgeous body curled up on her bed, ready for sleep. "Go to sleep, sweetheart," he crooned. "You're worn out . . . we both are!" he added wickedly. "I'll call you before you leave for work."

She sat up, at attention. "James, I—"

"Don't give me any arguments, Crissy," he interrupted. "Just go to sleep and dream of me, mmm? It's only fair that you do, because I'm surely going to dream about you," he added. "Oh, baby . . . what I'd give to have you here right now," he whispered, causing showers of goose bumps to cover Crissy's flesh. His voice trailed off when he got caught up in his own fantasy, then he abruptly cleared his throat. "I'll talk to you in a few hours, honey."

"Good night, Mr. Prince," she said, her mind in a fog, her body in a dither.

"You know, whenever you make that Freudian slip

of using formal language, I always know I got closer than you wanted me to be, Crissy," he theorized. "Don't be afraid of me, honey. Trust me. I'll never hurt you. I promise."

She whispered good-bye and quietly hung up the phone, still unsure whether his feelings were strictly emotional—*sexual*—or if he was beginning to love her as she surely loved him. Then she galvanized her body into action when she glanced at the clock and realized she had less than two hours to make her flight.

Hurriedly, she showered and dressed in a light gray business suit, pinning a red silk rose on the wide lapel. She gathered together her makeup and an extra crush-proof blouse and packed them into her small overnight bag, found her keys and changed purses. Next she called her boss at Silver Dollar City, leaving a message on his answering machine that she wouldn't be in that day. Then she checked to be sure all the lights were out and the windows and doors locked. The last thing she did was reset her answering device before she flew out the door into the pale dawn light.

She made the flight with some time to spare. The highway had been almost deserted, and it was only a little over fifty miles up Highway 65 to Springfield from her summer home, so the drive had taken just an hour. She was able to sleep a little on the short hop to St. Louis, and she felt quite refreshed when she stepped from the plane, at once spotting her friend Jack at the end of the long passageway, waving his greeting. His dark good looks made him stand out in the crowd.

"Belle," he called, closing the distance between them with long, sure strides. He caught her up in a warm embrace and kissed her on her full parted lips, holding her and the kiss longer than was necessary, Crissy thought. "It's so damned good to see you again," he murmured, smiling broadly when he released her.

"It's good to see you, too." She *was* glad to see him, and his kiss had been very pleasant . . . still, she hadn't seen any skyrockets. "What's up?" she asked, putting her small case in Jack's willing hand and beginning to walk alongside him to the exit.

He quickly explained the situation, telling her that a new product line was going to be launched three months earlier than originally planned and the decision had changed his agency's production schedule in the process. "It's a commercial for a new breakfast cereal, Belle," he went on. "Name: Scoops O' Crunch; voices needed: a giggling little girl, a frisky puppy, and a jubilant, chirping bluebird. Think you can do all three?"

"I can try, Jack." She smiled when the lines of tension melted from his handsome face.

"Thatta girl!" he said with approval. "If we work like hell today, we can have dinner together before you take the red-eye back tonight. We haven't spent any time together since that commercial last spring," he complained. "I've missed you . . . terribly."

She laughed at his theatrics. "Don't pull that little act with me, friend," she teased. "I've never known you to be without the company of an attractive woman whenever you snapped your fingers. Handsome ad men like you never have any free time in their date books. You're just trying to make me feel guilty," she accused, a knowing smile on her face.

"Can't blame a guy for tryin'," he tossed back lightly, helping her into his car and climbing behind the wheel.

Most people outside the ad industry were not aware of the hard work that went into a thirty-second or sixty-second commercial. Crissy knew the television viewer or the radio listener had little insight into the business, never realizing the time and effort and perseverance it took to make a short commercial message entertaining but informative. The bottom line was: Make the message palatable, but make the consumer listen . . . and act upon the information.

She had learned a great deal in the five years she

had been in the business of doing radio commercials and lip-synching television voices, and her work was professional—she never wasted time and always listened to direction.

Sometimes the producer or the director would become frazzled, trying to suggest the tone of voice they wanted or the type of personality needed for the speaking part. When that happened, more often than not, Crissy would invent what was needed on the spot, and the producer would exclaim, "Belle, you're a mind reader! It's just what we want." Then their frowns would disappear and Crissy would feel very satisfied with herself. Yes, this business was gratifying. She loved it and hoped she could work in the field for many years to come.

Jack opened the door of the recording studio, and Crissy was welcomed with open arms by the producer, the director, and the audio engineer—all old friends. She slipped off her suit coat and hung it around the back of her chair, then sat down, ready to be briefed on her roles. Listening attentively, she scanned the script while Missy, the director, cued her to their needs. Within an hour Crissy had supplied the right voice for the chirpy bluebird and produced the correct, happy-sounding bark of the puppy, but the voice for the giggling little girl, the part that really carried the message of the commercial, seemed to elude her.

Again and again she tried one voice after another, noting her listeners shaking their heads as they huddled around her with their eyes closed, listening raptly. Suddenly all four people jerked their heads upright, eyes wide opened, as they shouted in unison. "That's it, Belle! Say the words in that voice again."

She did as they requested, putting every bit of her training into her work, speaking clearly and distinctly in the newly invented child's voice. When she giggled happily at the end of her words, punctuating the message with joy, they all nodded in agreement.

"By Jove, I think she's got it!" crowed Jack in an

outlandish, affected British accent. And Crissy giggled in her little girl's voice again, giving everyone in the room an opportunity to let off steam after the intensity of the last three hours. They decided to have a coffee break before getting down to the actual business of recording the commercial, which might take several hours. More than once, Crissy and the crew had worked until the wee hours of the morning, recording and rerecording a single thirty-second commercial. That was the part she wished the consumer could see—how hard everyone worked to make an effective commercial.

She and Jack decided to walk along the long, glass-walled corridors as they sipped their coffee and munched on some sample granola bars for quick energy. They paused at the corner to look out over the city below. St. Louis was on the move again after a long economic decline. Crissy took pride as a Missourian that this fair city now led the nation in commercial building contracts, and the advance was clearly evident as she scanned the skyline.

"Back to the salt mines, my darlin'," Jack said after a few moments. He turned and started walking. Crissy matched his stride and tucked her arm under his in a friendly fashion. He glanced down at her smiling upraised face and leaned quickly to kiss her lips, whispering, "Belle, give me a chance to show you how much I could care."

She kept walking, knowing he was serious, but unable to answer right away. She had to keep it light for both their sakes. The image of James's handsome face swam before her eyes. She would not treat Jack shabbily. "You're one of my best friends," she said softly. "I'd like to keep it that way."

"Like I said, Belle the beautiful. You're some kinda lady!" he replied, swiftly covering the heart he had pinned to his sleeve and grateful that she hadn't made fun of his declaration. "Work! That's what we need. Then dinner in a softly lit, intimate place I know, where I'll wine and dine you to distraction," he promised with a wicked smile. And they both laughed at his thinly disguised joke.

Two commercials lasting thirty seconds and one of sixty seconds had been completed to everyone's satisfaction when they called it a day. Actually, it was almost ten o'clock at night when Jack and Crissy sat down for their late dinner at Tony's, a downtown restaurant with an international clientele. Jack made no overtures or demands, and she was able to relax and enjoy the food, fine wine, and pleasurable conversation. He had a wry sense of humor and a ready wit that kept Crissy amused. She glanced at her watch a little later and announced that she had to go if she was to make her flight back to Springfield. Jack paid the check, and within the hour had her safely checked in and ready to board her plane.

"Thanks for giving me the opportunity to make this commercial," she said sincerely. "I hope it pleases your client."

"Thank *you* for doing such a great job, Belle," he replied, pulling her into his arms. "The client is going to be ecstatic," he predicted. "You're the best in the business, honey." He hugged her tightly. "I'm going to miss you . . . all through the night and tomorrow."

She laughed softly. "Jack, you look me straight in the eye and tell me you don't have a date for tomorrow evening with some great-looking woman," she demanded. When she saw his sheepish grin and flushed face, she smiled with satisfaction. "You'll miss me like you miss having a mother-in-law!" Then she kissed him on the cheek and said good-bye. She could hear his hearty laughter all the way down the corridor to the plane.

The drive home took longer than the flight from St. Louis to Springfield. Crissy was exhausted when she arrived at her cabin. It was almost three o'clock in the morning, and she had to go to work today. She and her boss had an understanding; she would sometimes have to leave on short notice for such jobs. She hadn't told him exactly the nature of these jobs, but Jeff was an old friend and trusted her. He was also not someone who pried into her life. "As long as you're not gone more than one day a week, I can deal with it," he had told her the day he gave her the summer job. And she had promised she would try her best always to be on duty during the weekends, when the crowds were the largest. She had kept her word, and so had he.

Yawning tiredly, she slipped out of her clothes and absentmindedly reversed her answering machine to hear any messages she might have received. She was dumbfounded when she realized the whole tape was filled with James's deep, vibrant voice, growing more and more strident as his repeated calls indicated, first anger, and then worry.

"Good morning, sweetheart," purred the first call of the day. "It seems I've missed you, but I'll tell your little machine anyway. I'm meeting you at work to take you to lunch. P.S. I had a gr-r-reat time yesterday." Crissy, clad in her lacy slip, curled up on her bed to hear more. A warm smile curved her full mouth as she listened to his throaty, sexy voice.

"Crissy, you aren't at work today," came the second call. His voice mirrored his evident agitation. "Call me at the office this afternoon." She heard the rather sharp click of his phone when he hung up.

The third call was angry. "Crissy Brant. *Where the hell are you?* If you're hiding or playing games with me, I swear I'll tan your hide, woman! Now, pick up that damn phone and call," he ordered, slamming the receiver down.

Crissy sat up now, her face revealing a grin of triumph but also a shadow of fear.

"It's now ten P.M. Crissy, where are you? I'm going out of my mind with worry. Please, *please*, call me, baby," said the next call. His voice was pleading. She wasn't certain whether it was fear for her safety or the fear that she was refusing to speak to him. Before she could decide, his voice came out of her recorder again.

"Crissy, it's midnight. I've just gone to the sheriff to report you missing. The damn fool just smiled at me—like I was a damn outsider!" he said explosively. "He claims you sometimes go out of town on short notice. And he refused to give me directions to your cabin. I would have socked him in the jaw if I wouldn't have ended up in a cell . . . and away from a phone. God help you when I get my hands on you."

Crissy began to worry in earnest now. What was she going to tell him when she called? There was no question that she would call him, but what was she going to say? He sounded livid. But he also sounded sick with worry.

The rest of the tape was filled with short announcements of the time. "It's twelve-fifteen. . . . It's now twelve forty-five. Crissy, please call me. I didn't mean any of the threats. I just have to hear your voice. I'd never hurt you, honey. One A.M. and all is *not* well!" The calls had continued at fifteen-minute intervals until the moment she had walked in the door of her home.

At three-fifteen the phone rang, right on schedule. Nervously she reached for the receiver, and whispered, "Five two one two." She said no more, and could hear James's agitated breathing as he waited for her message before he could record his. When it was not forthcoming, he gasped, "Crissy, is that you? I mean . . . are you really there, in the flesh?"

"Good morning, James," she replied. "I'm sorry you've been worried about me. I should have called you when . . . when . . ." What the hell was she going to say to him? "I should have called you when I knew I had to go see my Granny Brant," she said, plunging on. "I'm truly sorry. Will you forgive me?" she pleaded softly.

"Oh, Crissy." He groaned, feeling all the force of his anger and fear draining from his tense body. "I've been so worried . . . damn near out of my mind . . . and then I got mad as hell."

"So your recorded messages revealed," she interrupted. "I was at my granny's house," she told him.

"She called me again right before I went to work and complained that she wasn't feeling well and asked me to come up the mountain. She wouldn't let the neighbors take her to the doctor, so I just had to go, James. You understand, don't you?"

"Of course, you had to go, Crissy. But is she all right? Did you have to put her in the hospital?" he asked, shooting the questions at her.

"I think she was more lonely than anything," she replied. "I spent the day and evening with her. Then some of our kinfolk came by for a visit, and it was three o'clock before I got back home. Do you forgive me for not calling you?" she asked, nearly purring her request.

He relented. "Yes, I forgive you . . . if you promise never to do it again. God, Crissy, I think I've aged twenty years since the last time I spoke to you," he proclaimed, exhaustion breaking his voice.

Even though she hated lying, she chuckled appreciatively at his exasperated words. "Then you'd better take a double portion of vitamins—lots of E—and get to bed. You're going to have to be rested and full of vitality when next we meet," she promised. Her voice had dropped to a low, sultry level and she hoped she had been able to make his hair stand on end. She was fighting for his love.

He filled the line with a string of low expletives, making Crissy laugh at his frustration. "Dammit, woman, now I'll probably lie awake all night. After I take several cold showers, that is," he added pointedly. "You're driving me crazy!" he yelled. "I'm telling you, you'll drive me right around the bend pretty soon."

She couldn't resist goading him. "I'm a very good shifter."

"The next time I get you alone I can promise you I'll be in the driver's seat, my beautiful little tease," he shot back, wishing he had her in his arms that very instant. "You're going to think you've just been hit by a ten-ton truck!"

"Are you insured, James?" she parried. "We don't want to be wrapped up in litigation, now, do we?"

He chuckled in that deep, vibrant way that sent shivers of pleasure up and down Crissy's spine. He was enjoying her ready wit. "The only thing I want to be wrapped up in is your arms . . . and your legs . . . and your soft, hot, luscious body. . . . I want to feel—"

"Can we have lunch together today?" she interrupted, feeling her skin become heated and her loins throb with desire.

"Open the window, Crissy. You're beginning to breath heavily," he ordered drolly, getting his pound of flesh, enjoying the awkward position he had put her in with his suggestive phrases. "I have a business lunch tomorrow . . . I mean today, honey. I'll call you at six, but I'll expect you at the Mexican Sombrero at seven sharp this evening. Okay?"

She agreed, and then he shocked her with his parting words. "Tonight, we go hot all the way, woman. See you soon. And I hope you sleep as well as I expect to," he ended, hanging up in triumph when he heard her exasperated expulsion of breath.

Seven

Promptly at six o'clock that evening, Crissy's phone rang. She was ready for James's call. As soon as she returned from work, she had taped a crying infant on the recorder she used when she experimented with new voices. I have to try to find out what his feelings are, she excused herself, feeling pangs of discomfort at her deception.

"Five two one two," she answered in her telephone-service voice.

"Ms. Crissy Brant, please," James replied, his voice showing his aggravation at the difficulty in reaching her.

"One moment, pul-ease," she said, pushing the hold button. When she came back on the line, she was her fantasy sister-in-law, Billy. "Hello," she chirped. "Crissy Brant's residence. May I help you?"

"This is James Prince," came his crisp reply. "I'd like to speak with Crissy, please."

"Oh, Mr. Prince. This is Billy, Crissy's sister-in-law," she said in a bubbling voice. "I'm sorry, but Crissy isn't home from work yet. May I take a message?"

She heard a long, exasperated sigh over the line. "Please tell her to call me as soon as she gets home," he requested, his voice smooth and low . . . and not meant to be disobeyed.

"I'll be glad to, Mr. Prince," she said in a serious young voice. Then she prodded herself. If you're going to get any information, it's now or never, Crissy. So she gushed on. "Ah, Mr. Prince? Crissy has told me about you. It's very nice to be talking to you." Then she giggled as if she knew a lot more.

"I've heard something about you, too, Billy," he returned. "I understand you have a very busy husband and a pretty baby girl." Was he trying the same thing, she wondered?

"Oh, yes, Johnny is in sales, but I guess Crissy told you that, and my little girl is the nicest thing that ever happened to me, next to marrying my Johnny," she said, letting a caress flow into her words. "I'm very lucky," she added. "We're staying with Crissy until my husband comes home tomorrow. It gets so lonely when he's not around." Okay, *now*, she decided. "I'd like to welcome you to our community, Mr. Prince," she said in a pleasant, happy voice. "Crissy speaks of you often. I think she likes you." She giggled again. "I'm glad you've been taking her out some. She seems to enjoy your company."

"I like her, too, Billy . . . very much," he answered warmly. "Tell me, what's she been saying about me?" he asked, and he covered well his curiosity with the casualness of his tone. Why, that rascal, Crissy mused. He's trying to pump my sister-in-law!

A smile of pleasure crept into her voice. "Well . . . I don't want to tell tales out of school, Mr. Prince."

"James, please."

She giggled again, as if she were terribly impressed with his urbane manner. "Well . . . she did tell me that she likes you. And she told me that you sometimes have disagreements, but she wouldn't tell me what about—and it's really none of my business," she rushed on when she heard his low laughter. "Fact is, you're the first man I can remember she even spoke about at any length in the last few years. She dates a lot, but she loses interest. You must be very special if Crissy is dating you more than usual," she added, her voice warm and coy. "I've been hoping she would find someone whom she could like as much as the fellas usually like *her*. Do you enjoy her company?"

He chuckled softly. "Very much," he murmured. "Crissy is like a breath of fresh air. She's so beautiful and intelligent, Billy. Besides," he added, "I never know what she's going to do next. And it's been a long time since I've found myself guessing . . . about anyone. I just wish she'd give me her trust," he finished lamentably.

"She's had a lot of unhappiness in her life, James. And some people have tried to take advantage of her giving nature," she explained honestly.

"But I'm an honorable man!" he countered. "I've tried to get her to trust me, but I don't know what else to do. What do you think, Billy? You sound to me like a woman with a good head on her shoulders. How can I win her trust?"

"Well . . . you could—" she began, then pushed the button on her tape recorder, filling the air with the wails of a small infant. "Oh, Crissy, Junior, is awake," she cried, eager to get off the phone. The cries continued while, with the same young voice, she made soothing sounds to the tape. "Hush, baby. Don't cry. Mama's here, honey." The howling got louder, and she spoke over the noise. "James, I have to hang up now. The baby needs me."

"Wait! Don't go, Billy. You were going to tell me something," James called over the line.

"I'm sorry, James," she answered. "Perhaps we can talk again sometime. I have to go. 'Bye." And she dropped the receiver into its cradle.

"Whew!" said Crissy out loud as she turned off the tape recorder. That was close, she thought. I was just about to tell him . . . no, I mean Billy was about to tell him to tell me how he felt. Good grief! I think *I'm* the one who's being driven around the bend, she thought in confusion. Then she smiled to herself and hurried to begin dressing. He *had* said he liked her . . . very much!

Quickly she showered and returned to her bedroom. Dialing James's number, she had to wait just two rings before he picked it up. "James? It's Crissy. I was a little late coming home. I had some errands to run," she explained. "Will we have to cancel our date tonight?" she asked, since she really didn't know why he had called.

"Hi, sweetheart," he answered, happy to hear her voice again. "We will *not* be canceling our date, Ms. Brant. I just wanted to know if you'd allow me to pick you up this evening. Will you?" he asked, hoping she would begin to give him at least a little of her trust.

If Crissy could have had her heart's desire, if she could be sure of James's affection, she would have given him directions and told him they would be spending the night here. Instead she spoke with a whisper of promise in her words. "It's very near the time for our dinner, James," she countered. "I think it would be better if I just met you, as we planned. Billy and the baby are here and . . . I just think it would be better," she ended, lamely.

He sighed, obviously discouraged by her refusal. "All right, Crissy," he answered quietly. "I'll be waiting for you." And he hung up without another word.

Crissy was disgusted with her lies. She knew he had been disappointed, but she also knew she had to guard her privacy until she felt more certain of him. He could, if he wished, throw open the doors to the publicity hounds. If he got angry, he could hurt her . . . and she was honest enough to admit to herself that he could hurt her because she was falling in love with him. Why, oh, why did fear have to be a part of falling in love? And she knew the fear would stay with her until she could believe in him fully and completely. It was like the poster she had seen years ago in a "head" shop: "If I tell you who I am, and you don't like what you hear . . . then what will I do?" Yes, she mused, what would she do?

She shook herself and hurriedly dressed. Because tonight they were going to eat Mexican food, she decided to wear a full, gathered, tiered skirt in vivid red and a matching peasant blouse. She puffed up her sleeves and daringly pulled the elasticized neckline down over her smooth tanned shoulders, making a charming frame for her new tulip necklace, which she hadn't removed since James had fastened it around her neck. She fingered the sparkling ruby charm, smiling when she remembered their night of love. It seemed a hundred years ago.

"Pull yourself together, Brant," she cautioned herself, rushing now to finish her makeup, adding just a touch of blusher to her rounded cheekbones and rubbing a clear red gloss across her full lips. She had already applied subtle shades of eye shadow to her lids and several layers of mascara to her black lashes, bringing out the exotic gold in her deep brown eyes. If James wanted hot, he would get hot, she promised her mental picture of his handsome smiling face. We'll just see which makes him steam more . . . the chili peppers or me!

She looked at her reflection and struck a provocative Spanish pose, one arm curved above her tousled black curls and the other slithering along the side of her breast and hip. All she needed was a rose between her teeth! Raising her eyebrow in a smashing arc, her eyes snapped, and she gave a throaty laugh. Coming to her senses, she thrust her bare feet into strappy high-heeled shoes and berated herself for her bravado. "Damn, Crissy, you've got more guts than you've got brains!" She sprayed a mist of musky perfume around her body and fastened large gold loops in her ears.

The Mexican Sombrero was crowded with the last tourists of the season. It was easy to spot the popular restaurant, because near the door towered a twenty-foot plaster-and-wood tequila bottle, its sides dripping with multicolored fake rivulets of wax. She often wondered why the owners hadn't taken the last step and placed a huge, beacon-flamed candle in the bottle's neck—it would have made the giant landmark the most gauche eye-catcher in this tourist mecca. Anything to catch the Yankee dollar!

She got out of her car and walked toward James, who was standing by his low-slung sports car. He watched intently as the setting sun at her back outlined her figure. She was unaware of the enticing picture she was presenting; her eyes, her entire body, were only aware of James and his hooded gaze. Her sweeping glance took in his tight jeans, which molded his long muscular body with alarming accuracy, and his light- and dark-blue-striped polo shirt stretched across his broad chest and bulging biceps. His feet were spread slightly, bare in comfortable but expensive loafers.

Their eyes locked, sending heady messages back and forth. Without a word, James swept her into his arms and kissed her with shattering passion. She felt helpless under his mouth, and her body melted into his. "I thought so!" he muttered against her lips, his hands moving exploringly along her spine. "You don't have a damn thing on under this red flag!"

She pulled away from him, flabbergasted by his words. "I certainly do," she protested. Then her face turned the color of her dress, because she suddenly remembered she had forgotten her strapless slip. But, by heaven, she had on her red bikinis, so she stubbornly insisted, "I do!"

He roguishly began a visual journey down her length, the blazing sunset his willing ally. When his gaze returned to her challenging dark eyes, he chuckled appreciatively and replied, "You could have fooled me, lady. Come on, let's eat. I'm famished." He took her hand in his and led her into the dark interior of the campy restaurant. She heard the taped flamenco music, and chuckled.

"Boy, you sure can pick 'em," said the Tulip in her voice when she took in the red-checkered tablecloths and wax-covered bottles, their candles flickering shadows on the walls.

He murmured in her ear, a moment before he seated her at a corner table, "I sure can, baby. I sure can!" And Crissy knew intuitively that he was no more talking about the eating place than flying to the moon!

After they ordered, he spoke of his day, describing his noonday meeting with several buyers who had flown in to confer on ordering his toys. He was rightfully proud of the large orders they had made for spring sales. "People *do* want high-quality toys," he declared. "My determination to meet that need is going to pay off, Crissy—I know it."

"I always want the best," she agreed. "And if I can't have the best, I'd rather do without."

"We can agree on that," he said. "And when I see what I want, I go after it . . . regardless of the time and effort involved."

Crissy could not reply to that. He wasn't talking about toys or possessions any longer, that much she knew, and she was saved from an embarrassing lull in the conversation when the chattering waitress arrived with a trayful of Mexican fare.

At once they dove into the highly spiced food, washing it down with copious amounts of Mexican beer. When they dared each other to eat a whole chili pepper without flinching, each popped one into the mouth and glared across the table, chewing methodically while the tears streamed down both their cheeks. Finally neither could stand the heat a second longer, and they gasped for breath and simultaneously grabbed their frosty glasses of beer to put out the fire.

After she could speak again, Crissy became a Mexican temptress. "Thees ees ver-r-y tasty food, *señor*," she whispered, her eyes bright with tears, her voice sounding low and sexy when, in reality, it was only the hot peppers burning her mouth and throat.

His eyes teased her good-humoredly. "What is your name, little *señorita*?" he crooned, his voice, too, almost disappearing by the end of his question.

She quaffed her beer once more and replied in a singsong fashion. "My name is Chiquetta Margareeta Ernestita Teresita . . . Jones!"

He choked on her last name, and she rushed on, delighted she could make him laugh. "You see, *señor*, my papa, he was on hees way to the Tween Cities in Minneesoota, and he lost hees wa-ay," she said, letting her voice take on a lilting note. "He sets hees eyes on my mama and—Chihauhau!—he ees lost again . . . this time, in love . . . I thi-ink!" Her eyes snapped provocatively, and she casually adjusted the neck of her blouse, pulling it lower on her shoulders. "He always teese my mama, telling her he stay in May-hee-co because of the weather-r-r. Eet ees *so-o-o hot*, he say. But he was feeling the heet of mama's love . . . I thi-ink," she ended musically, lowering her eyes shyly, then lifting her lashes to reveal the heat of her gaze.

He was visibly shaken by her startling eyes, and Crissy smiled slowly, meeting his fiery gaze. He finished his beer and shook his head. "I think I know what your papa was feeling, little *señorita*. Let's get some air. I'm about to burn up in here," he mumbled, rising from his chair and throwing several folded bills on the table before he guided her through the crowded room to the door.

He took a long, calming breath when they reached her car, chiding himself for letting Crissy—little Crissy—get to him like that. But he lost all control again when he looked down into Crissy's wide, innocent eyes and heard her whisper, "Are you feeling better now, James?" in a crooning, maternal voice as she touched his cheek with her cool fingers. The lights flooding the parking lot, now that it was dark, did nothing for his composure when he glanced along her body and saw its shape backlighted—again!

He forced his voice to sound natural. "I think we could both use a cooling dip. What do you say?" he questioned, raising his eyebrow seductively. "Let's go home, honey."

She nodded without a word and dug into her small purse to find her keys, unlocking the door of her car. "I'll follow you," she told him, not quite meeting his intense gaze.

When they pulled into his driveway, James quickly walked ahead and turned on the front light. Then he came back for her, pulling her close to his side with his strong arm. "Whew! That was some food." He chuckled. "I still feel on fire."

"Maybe a dish of ice cream would cool you off," she suggested, moving along the hallway toward the living room and the pool.

"On top of all that beer?" He shook his head in vehement denial. "No. No more food. I'm looking forward to our swim. That's what I want to do," he said, leading her over to the couch.

"But it won't do any good," she said, pouting. "The water's heated."

"And you don't have your suit," he shot back wickedly, laughing when she burst out that she had completely forgotten it.

"Wait a minute!" she exploded. "I wasn't *told* to bring it," she remembered. "I was just going to have dinner with you."

But he cut off any more words she might have uttered, with a kiss so shatteringly sweet, she could only sigh and lean into him, meeting his demand with one of her own. His heated response to her actions sent them reeling onto the long, soft couch, where he continued to cover her skin with moist kisses. He trailed them along her throat until his mouth was against the soft rise of her breasts. Without a word, he began to pull the red blouse down to her waist, kissing her body as he revealed it. She moaned softly and arched against his mouth, digging her nails into the muscles of his shoulders.

"God, but I've missed you, Crissy, my sweet," he crooned, drawing the hard bud of one breast into his mouth, flicking and biting gently at the tender peak. "When your sister-in-law told me you hadn't returned from work, I was afraid you'd run away again," he said, burying his face in her softness.

His words brought her down from the ether. She had to regain some control of this situation, she told herself. "Yes, Billy told me you two had a long talk. I hope she didn't embarrass you. Sometimes she acts like the original matchmaker," she said, sitting up and straightening the bodice of her dress. "She won't be happy until every person she knows has somebody to call his or her own."

Quietly he rose to make a fire in the fireplace. When it was burning brightly, he pulled her up from the couch and held her in his arms, kissing her hair and running his fingers along her back. "No, she didn't embarrass me," he finally answered, giving her a kiss that took her breath away. "But she gave me some interesting information," he teased softly.

She had to play her part. "Now, what stories has that woman been telling you?" she asked, pretending surprise and anticipation.

He continued to hold her close, denying her access to the expression on his face. "She told me that you liked me . . . that it's the first time you've ever talked about any of your men friends . . . and this was also the first time you had dated a man more than a few times before you lost interest," he ended, a bit of pride creeping into his tone.

She pulled away from him, placing her hands on her rounded hips. "Why, that little stinker!" she exclaimed. "Wait till I get my hands on her." But there was a smile in her threat.

"Now, don't get yourself all in a dither, Crissy," he

said soothingly. "It was my fault. I pumped her unmercifully. You see, I was trying to find out how you *did* feel."

She refused to confirm or deny her feelings for him. She needed to hear, from his own lips and face to face, what *his* feelings were. "And if I know my sister-in-law, she did her share of wheedling, too," she said. "What did you tell *her*?"

"I told her I like you . . . very much, Crissy," he answered in the same quiet tone. Then he whispered, "What I didn't tell her—what I didn't realize until I saw you again this evening—is that I've fallen in love with you." He sighed now that he'd said the words. "Who would have thought a little mountain gal could bewitch me and steal my heart so fast? A woman with a crazy sense of humor, and well-educated," he hastened to add, "but a country girl nonetheless. And with a stubborn streak a mile wide!"

She stood transfixed at his words. Tears misted her vision, bringing a halo of light around his tanned handsome face; the golden lights in his thick hair and moustache seemed to glisten. She couldn't speak. Her emotions were too near the surface.

He sensed her turmoil and brought her close into his arms again. Both could feel the blaze of the logs and the heat of their desire. Tenderly he tipped her chin so he could look deeply into her sparkling eyes. "The question," he murmured, his voice low and serious, "is whether you'll trust me with *your* heart, Crissy. Can you?"

She tried three times to speak, and finally got the words out. "I don't know." She moaned softly, her voice breaking. "Everything is happening so quickly."

"I realize we've only known each other a short time," he agreed, continuing to hold her against his strong body, smoothing her curls from her troubled brow. "But, Crissy, you know we're good for each other. You've felt what we have together," he continued. "Trust me, darling. Give me a chance . . . give *us* a chance," he said earnestly.

His words touched her heart. She looked up into his deep blue eyes, letting him read her thoughts. "I love you, James," she whispered, almost too softly to be heard, but the smile that spread over his face, the light coming into his eyes, told her he had heard her words.

His kiss was so sweet and gentle that the tears that had threatened, spilled down her cheeks. He kissed each salty trail, covering her face with his touch, giving poignancy to the moment. "My darling Crissy," he crooned. "I'll never hurt you. I promise." His passionate mouth covered Crissy's and sealed the commitment.

It was almost dawn before Crissy left. They never did have their relaxing swim. James wanted to follow her home, but she refused, this time because he looked so tired and had a full day of meetings planned. She promised him she would bring him to her home in the evening. When she reaffirmed her promise to trust him, he reluctantly gave in. Then he gave her a key to the gate and his home, "so you can come and go as you please." She drove home in a daze of happiness, knowing she had made the right decision. "I love him. I love him," she shouted. "And he loves *me*!"

The next morning, promptly at eight, the phone rang. Crissy knew it would be James, wishing her a good morning and a good day. Her impish humor prodded her to have one more fantasy phone conversation with him. This time Granny was going to talk to him. Tonight she would confess everything, and they could both have a good laugh over her deception. Actually, she told herself, it had all ended up as harmless fun. James would see that too.

She picked up the phone. "Five two one two," she said in her answering-service voice. Then, when James asked for her, she pushed the hold button and came back on as Granny Brant. "Howdy!" she said, holding back the giggles that threatened to ruin her act. "Who's this?" she prodded in a gruff, old voice.

For a moment James said nothing. Shock, she supposed. She heard him clear his throat and ask politely, "This is James Prince. May I speak with Crissy, please?"

She filled the room with cackling chuckles. "Well, it's about *time* I talked to you," she said in a no-nonsense voice. "Jimmy, this here is Crissy's granny. She ain't here right now. She went to fetch some things fer me afore she went on to work this mornin'," she explained in a wizened voice. "Jist as well she's gone, cuz you and me got some talkin' to do, young feller."

She tried to picture James's grim face, getting himself ready for the third degree he knew was coming. "Hello, Mrs. Brant," he greeted her, his voice warm and friendly. "Crissy has told me quite a lot about you. I hope you're feeling better," he added solicitously.

Crissy grinned, but she answered gruffly. "I'm finer'n frog hair, Jimmy! Fit as a fiddle! And you'd best be callin' me Granny. Everybody does," she ordered firmly.

"Granny it is," he replied, ready for her next volley.

"What's this I hear 'bout you and my granddaughter?" she cut in, warming to her role. "I reckon my shotgun and me kin still take care of you ifen yore intentions ain't honorable," she said boldly.

"My intentions are strictly honorable," he hastened to say. "I care a great deal for Crissy, Mrs. . . . Granny. I want only what's best for her."

"And is you fixin' to be what's best fer her?"

"I hope so . . . I know so!" There was strength in every word, and Crissy hugged herself with delight.

"Well . . . I reckon she's old enuf to know her own mind," Granny said. "But you'd best remember, she's got a heap of kinfolk in these hills, and ifen you don't do right by her, we'll take care of you," she threatened darkly. "I loves that little gal like she ware my own, and *nobody messes with my Crystabelle!* Hear?" she croaked out, dropping the bombshell of her full name in the process.

She heard his gulp of disbelief loud and clear. "Crystabelle? Did you say her name was *Crystabelle*?" He laughed suddenly, making Crissy bridle. She gave him a one-liner she had been dying to use since she'd first thought of it, years ago.

"What's a matter, sonny?" she yelled. "Crystabelle be a *fine* name." Then she chuckled as sexily as an old woman could. "After all, young feller, she rings yore chimes, don't she?"

His surprised reply sounded choked out. "As a matter of fact, she does, Granny. And . . . incidentally, I love her, too."

Crissy could not contain her happiness at his words. She had to hang up. "Take care of her, sonny," she managed to say and broke the connection. She fell across the bed, laughing happily, wishing she could see the look of incredulity that must be on his face at this very moment.

By 8:30 she was on the road to Silver Dollar City. She couldn't resist pulling in at a roadside phone to call James. "Hi," she said when he came on the line. "I'm just calling to say good morning, since I missed your call earlier," she began, stopping for a moment when a huge truck went rumbling by. "What did you say to Granny? She was chuckling and happy as a lark when I returned with her yarn."

"I told her that I loved you."

"She didn't say anything to upset you, did she?" she asked cautiously.

"It would take more than a 12-gauge shotgun to keep me away from you, baby," he murmured sensuously.

"Oh, my!" she lamented. "James, she still operates by the code of the hills."

"But she knows my intentions are honorable," he countered. "I promised to take care of you . . . Crystabelle!" He chuckled, waiting for the explosion.

"Oh, no." She moaned in feigned horror.

"Now, sweetheart, you have a fine name," he said, repeating Granny's words. "And, besides, you *does ring my chimes!*" he teased. "Yes, siree, bob, I been hearin' bells and whistles and gongs since the first time I kissed you, honey," he told her, joining in her laughter now.

"I'm going to be late for work, James," she replied, catching her breath. "I'll talk to you at six tonight."

"Er, Crissy, haven't you forgotten something?" he prodded gently.

She knew what he wanted to hear. "I love you, James," she whispered.

"Ahhh, those words fill me up better than a pancake-and-sausage breakfast." He sighed. She wanted to scold him for thinking of food again, but he hurriedly added, "And the cardinal says, 'Have a good day,' my love," giving words to the redbird in the art-glass kitchen door. " 'Bye, sweetheart."

Crissy's day was magnificent. She didn't see a cross tourist; she didn't hear a crying baby. Everything was wonderful as she told her stories to the crowds and made them laugh at her stories and chuckle at her antics. She could do no wrong.

All's right with my world, she thought, rejoicing, as she drove up to her little cottage running around in the yard before she skipped up the steps to the porch. When James called, she had already bathed and was curled up in her soft robe on the bed.

"Would you like to come to my home for the evening, James?" she asked, keeping her promise to trust him. "I'd like to spend our time here tonight . . . I have some stories to tell you," she murmured, also keeping her promise to herself to tell him everything.

James groaned as if he were in real pain. "Damn!" he said beneath his breath. "Of all times!"

"Don't you want to come?" she interrupted, aware of his agitation.

"Honey, there isn't any place I'd rather be than

with you tonight," he declared. "This is the first time you're putting your trust in me. I've been waiting for so long for this invitation—"

"But?"

"But Tom Sinclair just dropped out of the sky this afternoon," he told her. Tom's name brought her right off the bed. "He took a detour on his flight from L.A. to New York just so he could have a face-to-face meeting with me. God, honey! I don't know what to say. His timing is awful . . . but I can't tell him just to take off. He's gone to so much trouble to get here," he said in exasperation.

"I'm sure his wedding plans are very important to him, James. You've got to talk to him."

"No, this is company business," he said. "We're trying to hash out the national sales campaign for Prince Toys . . . and it's going to take all night. If we're lucky, we'll have some concrete plans mapped out for the coming year before I have to run him into Springfield to catch the connecting flight to St. Louis for the red-eye home. Crissy, you know that if there were any way I could hold him off, I would. You *do* know that, don't you?"

"Of course I know that, James," she answered soothingly. "Your plans are very important. And I suspect you have some sort of a deadline to meet."

"You have *no idea* how much planning goes into a campaign of this size, honey," he said grimly, and Crissy smiled silently because he thought of her only as a cute little actress and a mountain schoolmarm. He would know differently soon, she vowed. "And the worst of it is," James continued, "I seem to have my work cut out for me, even with Tom. He claims I'm going to have difficulty getting the person I want to do the commercials. But I'm determined to get a woman named Belle Grady," he proclaimed, shocking Crissy to her toes. "She's the best in the business. I don't know why I haven't met her. Our paths never crossed, I guess, but I know her work well. Every commercial she does is tops. And there's no way I'm *not* going to get her!"

"I'm sure you'll be able to convince her," she replied fondly, knowing he already had her . . . body, heart, and soul! "Once you make your feelings clear to your friend Tom, I'm sure he'll see it your way. Who could resist you?"

He chuckled warmly at her gentle chiding. "She can't be any harder to convince than you were, baby," he whispered.

"Go get 'em, tiger." She growled provocatively. "I'll talk to you tomorrow."

"God, I'm going to miss you, Crissy," he lamented. "I'd offer to come to you later, but I know as sure as I'm talking to you that this meeting is going to go on till the moment I have to take him to the airport. Can I have a rain check on the invitation, sweetheart?"

"A rain check—and a sun check and a moon check." She chuckled.

"How about a snow check?"

"Do you think the meeting will take *that* long?" she teased, feeling the warm breezes wafting in from the window.

"No!" he said explosively. "I'll see you tomorrow . . . no matter what," he promised. "I love you."

"I love you too," she answered, feeling her heart swell with the joy of knowing her love was safe in his hands.

Eight

The next morning, Saturday, dawned sunny and clear. Crissy rose early to watch the sunrise. This was the last weekend of business at the amusement park where she worked. On Monday she would move back to Springfield, to her apartment, so she could get ready for the new school year. She hoped James wouldn't mind driving in to see her. And, of course, they would have every weekend together at his lakefront home or in her mountain hideaway. They had not spoken of marriage yet. Crissy thought James would not want to wait very long. For that matter, neither did she! Whatever plans they made, she was certain they would be happy ones.

She glanced over at her alarm clock. It was just five. She could sleep longer, she knew, slipping back into bed and snuggling into her pillow, wishing James were here. Suddenly she sat up, a grin of pure delight creasing her oval face. "Well, why not?" she decided happily. *"I'll just go to the mountain!"* Quickly she showered and dressed for work, humming as she hurried, visions of James's happily surprised face dancing in her imagination. She ran out to her car, shouting, "Good morning, world," and laughed in delight when her loud greeting startled a pair of cardinals from the cedar tree near the drive.

When she drove into Branson, she stopped at the corner bakery and chose a dozen of the gooiest, most luscious-smelling doughnuts she could find. She carried the still-warm baked goods, together with a gallon of milk, back to the car, hopped in, and took off for James's house. The ride took little time; traffic was still light.

Should she unlock the door herself and sneak into his bedroom and jump on his bones? she asked herself, feeling brave. Or should she "ring his chimes?" she wondered.

Wisely she decided she would wait at his front door, because she had no idea how he would react to an uninvited body disturbing his sleep. There was so much they had to learn about each other, she thought, pulling quietly into his driveway and closing the car door with care. She *was* determined to surprise him. She had to ring the bell several times before the front door flew open. "Surprise!" she exclaimed, laughing like a child at his wide-eyed, sleepy face.

"What the . . .!" He squinted against the harsh morning light. His blue, thigh-length silk robe was thrown carelessly around his tall frame, barely closed at the front, and Crissy would have bet a hundred dollars he had nothing on underneath. She smiled at her wanton thoughts, and he finally came out of his sleep-filled stupor and recognized her. "Crissy!" he whispered. "What are you doing here?"

She excused his terseness, chalking it up to his groggy state. "I brought you something for your body," she teased boldly, lifting herself on tiptoes to kiss his surprised mouth. Then she stepped back and held up her tokens of love for his inspection. "Breakfast," she said, laughing. "I've brought you breakfast. Shall I serve it to you in bed, master?" she asked coyly.

He was suddenly wide awake. A frown—of displeasure, she thought—crossed his face. "Crissy, I wish you'd called me first," he stated, glancing over his shoulder as he tried to pull the door closed behind him. But his efforts were too little too late.

She glanced beyond his stiff frame. Large diagrams and blueprints were propped everywhere around the room. On the floor, crumpled sheets of paper were strewn about, and manuals of some sort were lying open near a model of a piece of machinery. A disturbing thought brought the taste of bile into her throat, but she laughed nervously, and hoped with all her heart that the nagging suspicion could be put to rest.

She forced her voice to sound relaxed and a bit conspiratorial. "Ah, what do we have here? Am I the first to see your top-secret toy for the spring line?" She prayed she was right, but his reply instantly destroyed her assumption.

"No," he answered abruptly. For a moment he looked very uncomfortable. Then he straightened his shoulders and calmly explained. "It's a prototype for an automated line I want to install at the factory. If it's successful, the changes will increase productivity."

"And *decrease* jobs for the people of Branson," Crissy cried. "James, how could you?"

He swore beneath his breath when he saw her shocked features. "I can explain," he told her in a low, harsh voice. "Trust me."

She pushed past his unyielding body and strode angrily into the room. In exasperation and disgust, she picked up one, then another, of the charts and drawings. After glancing at the meticulously detailed plans, she dropped them with revulsion and turned on James. Her flushed face and defiantly clenched fists told him she was going to fight him on this, and he braced himself. There was nothing he could do about it right now. He realized her emotional response was going to be in defense of her friends and neighbors—her people. And, although she would be embarrassed when she got the story straight from him, still he'd have to let her blow off steam first.

"Trust you?" Her voice was filled with disdain. "You expect me to trust you, when it's obvious you're planning to automate your factory and throw men and women out of their jobs? People with families to support?" She shook her head angrily and cut the air with her next words. "You ask too much!"

Miserable at her discovery of James's intentions, she shoved the milk and doughnuts at him and turned to leave. "Good-bye, Mr. Prince."

Hurriedly he put the food aside and spun her around in his arms. An understanding smile at her protective attitude creased his rugged features. "You'd better let me explain, baby. If you don't, you're going to hate yourself in the morning," he teased lightly.

"I'm going to work!" Right now she didn't even want him to touch her.

"Not before we get this thing straightened out," he vowed. "You've got all kinds of crazy ideas running around in that head of yours, and they're all wrong, Crissy, *all wrong*."

She stood her ground and glared into his determined face. Her eyes were snapping with disappointment and anger. "All right. I'm listening."

He took a relieved breath and began. The explanation was so simple, really. She would laugh with him when she realized all the energy she had wasted because she had jumped to the wrong conclusion. "The machinery I plan to install will automate the packaging process only. It has nothing to do with the handcraftsmanship of the products, nor will jobs be sacrificed because of it." He smiled again, waiting to see her blush with embarrassment now that she understood. But instead of an apology, he reeled under the contempt in her reply.

"Sure you will, James. Production will soar when

you can switch more workers into the manufacturing section. But what happens in six months, when you decide a machine can do some of the simple assembly jobs faster? And what happens a year from now, when you make the decision to automate fully? I'll tell you," she said emphatically.

"You'll go to work each morning to an empty, unpeopled factory. You'll press a button at one end and your cute little toys will be spit out at the other. Oh, yes, your production and sales will sky-rocket, no doubt. But you'll have sacrificed the hand-crafted quality of your toys to *speed* . . . and you'll have destroyed the hopes and dreams of your discharged workers—my friends! They'll be back on the unemployment lines," she ended in total disgust.

Disconcerted by Crissy's outburst, he pushed his hand through his rumpled hair and sighed despairingly. "You just won't try to understand. Look, I haven't had any sleep in the last two days. I spent the rest of last night, after I took Tom into Springfield, poring over these plans. I had just dropped off when you began ringing the bell. Crissy, you've got to trust me on this. I have no intention of automating my production. I just want to free that group of skilled crafts people who are stuck in the packaging section. *That's all!*"

Crissy made no reply. She just stood frozen in his arms, glaring at him. The look on her face—expressing the feeling that he was a loathsome interloper—made the last of James's patience snap.

He grabbed her by the shoulders and shook her. "I can see we're back to square one again, right, Ms. Brant?" he said angrily. "Your childish suspicions of an outsider, your lack of understanding, just won't give me the benefit of the doubt. The point being, you simply don't trust me," he shouted. "Don't you remember, I told you I love you?" he asked, feeling her body shrink from his touch.

Crissy began to tremble. She was close to tears when she answered him. "Yes, I remember you said you loved me. But do you remember when I told you we give outsiders enough rope to hang themselves? And right now I *don't* trust you," she shouted, the tears beginning to spill down her flushed cheeks.

"Then you don't love me," he returned grimly.

"No, I suppose I don't," she whispered miserably, all the fight leaving her body. He dropped his hands from her shoulders, and she turned to walk woodenly out to her car.

"Trust is a two-way street, Crissy," he said after her. "And trust is what love's all about. I won't beg for your understanding," he stated firmly, pride in his voice. "If you can't give it to me freely, then I want no part of it. All or nothing, Crissy. I'm that kind of guy."

She turned at her car and looked one last time through tear-glazed eyes, capturing James's proud stance at the door. An instant before her face crumpled, she nodded once to show she clearly understood his ultimatum, then climbed behind the wheel and drove away.

Throughout the morning, she performed in a fog of tumultuous emotions. Like a sleepwalker she plied her trade, giving laughter to the huge weekend crowds, not even aware of the words she was mouthing to bring these people such happiness. She put her heart on hold while she did her job. By noontime she had made her decision. Eagerly she found a phone and dialed James's number, knowing he would understand when she told him she had made a terrible mistake. She did love him. She did trust him.

Now that she'd taken the time to think, she realized he would never relinquish the authenticity of his products. He needed her friends. They were the last of a breed—hand-crafts people. And she believed his explanation about the packaging machine. It made sense to her too.

The phone rang incessantly; James did not answer. All the strength left Crissy's limbs. She began to feel frightened. What if she didn't get the chance to heal the rift between them? James was a proud man. He would die before he begged anyone for anything. "Dear God, please let him answer. I *must* apologize."

Finally, she hung up the phone and stood staring at the dial. Hot tears scalded her face. He told me he loved me, she reminded herself, but the words did little to ease the pain in her chest.

She scrubbed her face, smearing her painted-on freckles and rosebud mouth unmindful of the forlorn spectacle she had become. Just then her sister-employee, the soap-making lady, came by.

"Hey, Crissy, how ya doing, honey?" the older woman asked pleasantly. Crissy jerked her head up to stare at her friend as if she suddenly realized where she was. A frown appeared on the woman's face. "What's wrong, my dear?" she probed. "You look like you've just lost your last friend."

Crissy smiled weakly and raised her hands and shoulders in resignation. "That bad, huh?"

"You'd better come along with me," the woman ordered, gently. "Your makeup needs a major overhaul." She led Crissy to the employees' locker area. She busied herself mopping up the evidence of Crissy's tearful episode, quietly soothing her with maternal words of wisdom. "I suspect these tears are part of a lovers' quarrel, right?"

Crissy dolefully nodded in reply.

"Is it the man I met the other day?" she interrogated, kindly. "You two seemed to have something special between you."

Crissy sniffed loudly. "We did, Sarah. But I've hurt his pride . . . I'm not sure I can ever get him to forgive me," she lamented.

Sarah continued reapplying Crissy's makeup as she spoke, quietly but firmly. "Pride can be an awful thing, honey," she agreed. "Sometimes it can get in the way of love and trust."

Crissy shuddered when she heard Sarah's last

word—trust. If she had trusted James, as she knew she should, his pride would never have become an issue. But she was so conditioned to suspect newcomers that trust, her kind of lifetime-and-forever trust, was not given easily. She only hoped she could find a way to convince James of her mistake. She should have realized his love for her was strong and deserved her love—and trust—in return.

Sarah did not delve into Crissy's problem any further. She seemed to know the young woman had to work it out for herself. Instead she patted her shoulder and gently pushed her out the door. "Go to work, honey. You'll find the way back into his heart," she predicted. "Love—true love—will always find a way."

Crissy gave the older woman, wise with her years in the world, a hug and a watery smile of gratitude. "Thanks for your faith, Sarah . . . and your help," she said, pulling her shattered emotions together and marching herself back into the crowds. The afternoon's work dragged on. Crissy thought the day would never end. Finally, she returned home and rushed to her cottage. Feverishly she rewound her answering machine, hoping with all her heart to hear James's voice. Her anguished groan of disappointment told the chirping birds at her window that he had not tried to reach her.

She grabbed the phone and dialed his number as quickly as her trembling fingers would allow. On the first ring she cleared her throat, ready for speech. On and on it rang. Finally, on the twentieth ring, she was forced to admit no one was going to answer.

"His office," she exclaimed, grasping at straws. She felt impelled to speak to him. But her disappointment was reinforced when she got a recorded message telling her the office was closed for the weekend and asking callers to call on Monday morning after 8:30. "*Damn recorder!*" she yelled, slamming down the receiver. Now she knew how frustrated James must have felt the night he tried to reach her.

Thus began her determined attempts to reach

James. Every fifteen minutes she dialed his home. In between calls she took a warm shower and changed her clothes. She made herself a sandwich of cold cuts and cheese slices, then barely picked at it. Night fell, and still she got no answer. Her head was beginning to throb from the incessant ringing of his phone. When she could stand it no longer, she grabbed her purse and slung it over her shoulder and rushed from her house. Fishing her keys out of the depths of her pouch, she threw herself behind the wheel of her little red car and gunned the engine, raising dust and gravel in her driveway.

She drove among her beloved hills, unmindful of the direction she took. It was not surprising, however, when she found herself at the gate of James's property. She opened the heavy lock and pushed the barrier to the side. She left it open. Her mind had gone on automatic pilot now, and she didn't consider the wisdom of her actions. After the short drive through his property, she pulled into his paved driveway and stopped, turning off the engine. Her tearful glance showed no lights in the house. Was James already in bed . . . or was he gone?

"My God, what have I thrown away?" she cried, reliving the moments she had spent in his arms. She threw herself from her car, slamming the door hard in her frantic effort to reach the house. She stumbled along the path; the only light came from the multitude of stars and waning moon above. She felt along the side of the door for the bell button, found it, and pressed again and again in her hysterical need to see James. He just *had* to be home, she prayed. Oh, please, let him answer, and she'd beg him to forgive her.

But the house continued to echo with the repeated chiming, and no one came to the door. She sobbed openly now. *James, where are you?* she screamed silently from her heart. *I need you. How can I reach you?*

A new thought came into her whirling mind. She

stood still, considering the repercussions of such an action. Do I dare? Yes, she decided, and pulled from her purse the key to his door. With fumbling fingers she slipped the key into the lock and felt the door swing open. She reached inside and flipped on the light switch, flooding the interior with warm yellow light. Hesitantly she stepped over the threshold and called in a quivering voice that didn't even sound like her own, "James? James, are you here? It's Crissy. I have to speak with you. James!" she whimpered, her words cried softly now. "Oh, my love. Where are you?"

She did not feel the persistent tug of her conscience at her right to be there as she walked woodenly into the house. She trudged about with unseeing eyes until her gaze fell on the long white couch in the living room. She pictured again their last evening together, and her heart contracted in self-inflicted pain. Her feet carried her to the den. A bittersweet smile of recollection curved her lips when she remembered their first night of love. Would she ever know his passionate kisses again? Or was it too late? Feeling tormented, she continued into the master bedroom and stood crying hysterically at the foot of the wide bed. Like a thief she stealthily lifted the corner of the cream quilt, hoping to see the red satin sheets again. Her cry of despair filled the empty room. They were gone. Had it all been a dream? she wondered dazedly.

Finally she stumbled to the charming country kitchen. She stepped to the back door and flipped up the outside switch, flooding with light the art-glass window in the carved wood. She took several steps backwards, until she was leaning against the long counter. Her eyes filled with tears again as she absorbed the beauty of the sparkling design. "Oh, redbird," she whispered. "Sing a song for me. Let him be reminded of me when he looks at your vibrant red hue. Let him remember the love we shared. *Let him know I love him.*"

Crissy had no idea how long she stood gazing at

the lighted window. Time had lost its meaning for her now. But a last idea had filtered into her consciousness during that trancelike time, and she dug into her purse again, looking for paper and pen to write James a note. Sitting at the table after she had found what she needed, she pondered the words she would write.

"Dear James, We must talk," she wrote simply. "Crissy." She propped the note against the lazy Susan in the center of the round oak table and placed the keys he had given her in front of it. It was difficult for her to leave the keys, but she knew that, in moments of weakness, she might be tempted to return again and again to this place where her love had blossomed. If James could not forgive her, then she never wanted to come here again. She could not stand the pain.

The strength of her decision forced her to get up and turn off all the lights before she closed the door behind her, hearing the ominous click of the lock before she stumbled back to her car to drive home.

Sleep eluded her that night as she lay beneath the cool covers and listened to the nocturnal sounds of the insects and small animals in the woods beyond. Sunday, the last day of the summer season, passed in a blur as she walked among the milling crowds and acted out her skits during the shows. Her professionalism and pride in her craft would not allow her to shortchange her audiences, but she had to admit, her heart wasn't in it. That part of her was in limbo, waiting for James to contact her.

She refused repeated invitations to a closing party of employees that evening and, instead, hurried home to check her tape recorder. She had little hope that he had called, because she had tried to reach him all day during her breaks and even during some stolen moments. Her greatest fear was confirmed—the tape was blank.

She took only three bites from her supper—a cold sandwich again—and finally sobbed herself into a fitful, nightmare-ridden sleep. She tossed about on her bed, crying out James's name, whimpering for his forgiveness. In the morning the dark shadows beneath her large brown eyes showed the depth of her despair. Her mirrored image stared back lifelessly, and she tried to face the fact that James had closed the door and locked her out of his life. She would try one last time to reach him, she decided, her will to reach him pushing aside, for the moment, her shattered emotions. She dialed James's home, methodically counting the rings until she had to face the obvious—he was not there. Then she dialed his office number, and was jolted from her confused state when a young woman with an eastern accent answered.

"Prince Toys," she said in a bright, Monday-morning voice. "Good morning. May I help you?"

Crissy jerked her head up and simultaneously cleared her throat. "I'd like to speak with Mr. Prince, please," she requested.

"I'm very sorry, but Mr. Prince isn't in the office today," came the answer. "May I take a message?"

Ignoring the woman's question, Crissy plunged on. "Is there another number where he can be reached?"

"I'm sorry, miss. He left no other number," she told her. "If you'll leave your name and number, I'll see that he gets the message when he returns," she offered.

Crissy gave the information, feeling as if she were losing her grip on the last lifesaving object in the storm-tossed sea of her future. "Please tell him that it's very urgent." Then she carefully replaced the receiver in its cradle.

Feeling like a zombie, she forced herself to begin packing for her move back to Springfield. It was hours before she carried all her belongings out to her car and stuffed them haphazardly into the small trunk and back seat. Finally, at three in the afternoon, the task was completed, and she walked around her summer home, checking to make sure all the windows were securely locked and the back door bolted tight. Her last chore was to call the phone company in Springfield. Before she did this, however, she tried one last time to reach James at his home. There was no answer. He must be refusing to answer his phone so he wouldn't have to talk to her. She began to cry again, softly and quietly. Some part of her was a little surprised she still had tears to shed. Then she called the Springfield office to turn on her phone there.

With one last look around her hidden retreat, she pulled the door shut and drove back to her apartment. One question kept running through her mind. Why did he refuse to answer her messages? He'd had three days to get back to her. My God, she thought, I must have hurt him too much.

It took her two days to get settled in her comfortable apartment. Actually, she had no energy to unpack her bags and stock the shelves. All her strength was wrapped up in thoughts of James.

Her mountain cottage near Branson was rustic and filled with the possessions that had lasted past her Granny's lifetime, while her quarters in the city were a little more modern. The apartment was almost as small, with the living room and bedroom decorated in Early American style, a postage-stamp-sized, white-and-red kitchenette, and a poppy-papered bathroom. But the view from her front windows only revealed a few trees and the street beyond. Crissy didn't particularly like living in town, but her weekends back at the cottage made the weekdays bearable. Besides, she was home very little, spending most of her time at the school, including many evenings when her students were rehearsing a play or preparing for their regional speech competition. Then, there were the high-school football, soccer, basketball, and baseball teams to support, depending on the season. In addition, she took advantage of the symphonic and fine-art programs that were available. Yes, she could fill her time during the week, always knowing she had the weekends to escape—home.

On Thursday, Crissy decided it was time to visit the school. Her part-time classes were due to begin in two weeks, and she had to check out her room and supplies. She already knew she would be teaching the first three days of each week, and could plan accordingly. Today she was dressed casually, in jeans, a beige sweater, and a tan cord jacket. She had completely forgotten her red trademark this morning, and it was not until she was driving across town that she remembered. Fondly she fingered the ruby tulip through her sweater, smiling sadly, because this was one day when James's gift truly served its purpose.

It was four in the afternoon before she finally returned home. The phone was ringing incessantly when she unlocked her door. She flew to answer it, almost shouting, "Four-oh-three-two!"

"Belle, is that you? It's Tom Sinclair," came a harried male voice.

"Yes, this is Belle," she confirmed, suddenly feeling nervous. "What's up, my friend?"

He cleared his throat nervously. "I don't know exactly where to begin, Belle," he answered. "Oh, hell, I guess I'll start at the beginning. First, I just put James on a plane back to Missouri. Second, since I am aware, in this twisted, extended-family situation, that you've been seeing him, would you be willing to admit to me that your legal name is Crissy Brant?"

"It is," she murmured, quietly. "Grady was my married name . . . but it's also one I can use legally in my profession." What was he driving at? she wondered, a shiver of fear coursing through her. "You realize, of course, Tom, that this is confidential information," she warned him.

"Yes, *yes*," he agreed in agitation. "But damn it, Belle . . . Crissy . . . oh, hell! Damn it, do you realize what a sticky situation you've gotten me into, here in New York?"

Drawing on every ounce of her theatrical training, she asked in a calm voice. "What are you talking about, Tom? You're not involved."

"Not involved?" He almost screeched. "Try this on

for size—James has been burning up the lines to your country number for the last three days. All it does is ring, and all James is doing is getting angrier and angrier."

"He had the weekend to return my call," she argued stubbornly.

"He's been in New York," Tom shouted. "He didn't get your message until late Monday afternoon, and by that time you were gone. I don't care if you've moved back to Timbuktu, Belle, you've got to call him tonight."

"I'll think about it, Tom."

"You've got to promise me, Belle. I'm close to a nervous breakdown up here."

"All right. I promise."

"And you've got to tell him who you really are," he insisted.

"No, I won't do that, Tom. I told you once that he could hurt me . . . and in the present situation, he can," she argued.

"Look, I'll draw you a picture, okay?" he cut in. "James is insistent that you and only you will do his commercial voices. He's been badgering me for your number so he can tie up the deal himself. He claims I'm not trying hard enough! I'm caught right in the middle. Can't you see that? I've given him every excuse in the book—you're committed to other projects . . . you haven't been feeling well . . . you're just not interested—and nothing—I repeat, nothing—will satisfy him. His determination to have his own way is . . . awesome! There's no other word I can use to describe it."

"I've experienced that power firsthand, but he's not going to have his way on this one," she informed him. "It would be very unpleasant, to say the least." Her imagination was already conjuring the fury he would heap upon her head if he found out she was the Belle Grady he was seeking. She would rather die than face that wrathful man, she decided.

"All right, Belle," he replied. His voice was quiet.

He seemed to be giving up the fight. "Just promise me once again that you'll call him tonight."

"I promise," she agreed, and thanked him for his understanding.

"And I shall go to the nearest church, light all the candles in sight, and begin to pray for a miracle," he retorted. "The good Lord is the only one who can straighten out this mess!" he exclaimed. "Will you call me by tomorrow afternoon with your final decision, honey?" he asked in a soft, pleading voice. "The scripts are finished and we're on hold right now. We could do the taping on Saturday," he wheedled. "Talk to James, then sleep on it, okay?"

"Okay," she answered. "But it won't do any good. I'll talk to you tomorrow, Tom." She hung up the phone.

Nine

By evening, Crissy was a basket case. Her nerves were shot, and she had yet to speak to James. Like a trapped animal, she stalked back and forth within the confines of her apartment, pummeling a small cushion on the sofa, straightening an already level picture on the wall, all the while trying to come up with the words she would say to James. She knew with all her heart that she wanted to apologize to him, wanted to mend the hurt and ask for his forgiveness. But what words could heal the pain of their confrontation? Finally she could stand the suspense no longer. She glanced at the wall clock—it was just nine. James would be home by now. With no more reason to put off the inevitable, she gingerly picked up the phone and dialed his number. On the third ring, he answered.

"James Prince."

"James, it's Crissy." Her voice broke with emotion. Even the sound of his voice could set her on fire. "I under—" Oh, no! In her nervous state, she had almost made a slip. "I wondered"—she rushed on—"if you got my message to call me."

James cleared his throat. Was he nervous too? "Yes, Crissy, I got your message on Monday afternoon," he informed her in a firm, serious voice. "It would have been helpful if you had left a forwarding number, since you seem to have left the area. I suppose you're back in the mountains—somewhere else—getting ready for the new school year." His words dripped like water from a melting icicle. "Was there something you wanted?"

How could she get out the words? He was making it impossible. "I called because . . . because I wanted to apologize for the words we had the other day," she forced herself to say. "I realize you were hurt and angry, James. I'm sorry," she murmured, but it was her unspoken words that rang in her ears: *I love you. I want to spend the rest of my life with you. I need you.*

"Apology accepted," was all he said. There was a long silence on the line, and then he cleared his throat again and said, "It might have been for the best, Crissy. At least we both know where we stand now . . . and I'm very busy these days with the work on the new sales campaign. I really wouldn't have the time for a long-term relationship." He sounded so cold.

Crissy covered the mouthpiece of her phone an instant before her sob of misery rent the air. Was he glad to be free of her? Oh, God, she didn't know what to think. She swallowed the lump that had risen like a fist into her throat and asked calmly, "Have you been able to sign Belle Grady yet?"

He sighed unhappily. "No, dammit! She's an intolerable woman, that Belle. And as stubborn as they come," he added. Then he laughed in a deprecating manner. "But of course you and I have discussed her contrary nature before, haven't we?"

"Yes," she replied. She had to get off the phone before she broke down. "Well, I wish you luck in your endeavor, James," she said cheerily. "You once told me you always get what you want, no matter the cost."

He laughed harshly. "So it seemed . . . until recently," he countered. "You'll have to excuse me now if there's nothing else I can help you with. I have a great deal of work to do tonight."

When she told him she also had work to do, they both hung up after a very low, almost gruff, "Good-bye."

She sat next to the phone, staring blindly as the dark mantle of her aloneness and despair settled over her. She would never see him again, she realized sadly. Never would she know the warmth of his kisses, the passion of his touch. She should have listened to her heart instead of her head. She should have trusted him. Face it, you little fool, she told herself sternly, you didn't believe him . . . and now it's too late. She began to cry softly, unmindful of the tears dripping from her chin. "Oh, my love," she crooned, hugging her stomach. "If only I could take it all back. Make it up to you somehow. But it's too late."

She sat up half the night and drank an entire bottle of red wine, not even questioning her behavior. After passing out on the couch in an alcoholic stupor, she awoke at noon with a colossal headache that threatened to burst her skull and an upset stomach that made her queasy for the entire day. She chided herself unmercifully for trying to find solace in a bottle. She had never done it before and knew now she would never try it again. The results only added to the pain of James's rejection and her own feelings of foolishness.

All through the night and day of her personal crisis, she had been trying feverishly to think of some way to let James know how sorry she was. If only she could give him something that he wanted. She flew to her feet and began pacing around the living room. Of course! She would give him Belle. Of course, he'd never know *she* had done it . . . but she would! She hugged herself and smiled warmly for the first time in days.

After calling the airline, she ran into the bathroom and showered and shampooed her hair. The hot water streaming over her aching body soon washed away the last reminders of her solo drinking bout. Again she affirmed, "Never again!" Wrapped in a fleecy red robe, a thick terry towel twisted about her wet curls, she sat down at the phone and with trembling fingers dialed Tom's number in New York. Within moments, he was on the line.

"Belle, Belle," he cried in an anguished voice. "Please tell me you've come to your senses. Please, *please*, tell me you've told everything to James."

She laughed musically at his distress, knowing she was going to make him feel better. "The good news first," she said, the smile on her face evident in her words. "I'll fly in tonight and be ready to do James's commercials in the morning."

Before she could continue, Tom almost split her eardrum with his hoot of happiness. "Thank you, dear lady. My prayers have been answered. My life is saved . . . and also my job. James called me this morning and more or less told me that if I didn't cough up your number, I could start looking for another job, future brother-in-law or not. He said he'd see to it that I was fired."

"Oh, Tom," she said commiseratingly. "I *am* sorry. I didn't think he would act like such a child," she added in surprise.

"More like a bear with a sore paw," he countered knowingly. "Julie refuses to speak to him until he apologizes for ruining our dinner the other night. But you must realize he's so used to working like hell and getting what he wants."

Yes, she thought sadly, her heart breaking in her breast. He told me that too. "Well, he's going to get his way only because *I* changed my mind," she reminded him stubbornly. She could not see her own prideful behavior, it seemed.

"I hate to ask, Belle, but you *did* say something about bad news." He girded himself.

"Oh, it's not *that* bad," she chided gently. "It's just that James cannot know Belle is doing his blinking commercials . . . until I'm finished. You'll have to hold him off until Monday. Sunday, at the earliest."

"Would you like me to cut off my right arm and send it to you?" He groaned. "It would be easier, I can assure you."

"If you tell him you finally convinced Belle to work for him, you know perfectly well he'll hop the first plane east so he can have his fingers in the pie too," she explained patiently. "He's an adman, and old admen never die, they just—"

"I know, I know," he interrupted. "They just keep hoping for a Clio," he said, jokingly referring to the yearly awards for outstanding commercials.

She chuckled appreciatively. "Well, something like that," she replied, becoming nervous again. "Look, I'm leaving on the nine-fifty flight from St. Louis tonight. I'd appreciate it if you'd meet me at the airport with the scripts so I can study them before our meeting in the morning. Is that all right with you?"

"I'm with you every step of the way, beautiful."

"*Now* I get the compliments, huh? But, Tom, I'm serious about James being kept out of it. If you won't give me your word about keeping this whole thing a secret until after it's finished—and if you won't promise to keep my real identity a secret—then, just call it off. I won't come. *I mean that,*" she said, her voice as strong as steel.

"You've got it," he replied happily.

"Say the words, Tom," and she smiled in satisfaction when he repeated her words exactly, after which he sent her a kiss, with a promise to give her one for real at the airport. She hung up, laughing at his foolishness. Momentarily her heart contracted at the last trick she was going to play on James. But this was the only way she could give him his heart's desire—Belle. She could not face him again. For then *she* would be the fool!

Realizing there was no time for any kind of thinking right now—it was time for action—she hurriedly packed her suitcase with the outfit she would wear for the recording session, adding some nightclothes and her cosmetics. Then she dressed in her "uniform" for traveling—well-worn, comfortable blue jeans and a medium-weight red sweater, adding her warm rawhide jacket and hiking boots. There was no telling how chilly the weather might be in New York at this time of year, she decided. She was glad she had called to reserve a seat on the plane before she told Tom she would come. Time was growing short, and she was driving at the upper speed limit out to the airport, arriving minutes before her plane was scheduled to depart. The ticket agent, who was now an old friend and used to Crissy's nerve-shatteringly late arrivals, smoothed her path, insisting she could carry on her medium-sized bag and thrusting her tickets into her trembling fingers. She waved over her shoulder, laughing merrily when she saw the man shake his head in frustration at her latest close call.

When the plane arrived, just after midnight, she spotted Tom almost immediately. He gave her the promised playful kiss and twirled her around with joy. "Thank God you're here, Belle," he exclaimed, smiling from ear to ear. "For just an instant I was scared to death you'd changed your mind again."

"You gave me your word, Tom," she answered solemnly, "so I can keep mine."

"It's nice to know I can count on somebody," he returned gruffly. "I don't think Julie's ever going to come out of her lab long enough to marry me," he said sadly. "She's just like her brother. When they're mad, they bury themselves under a mountain of work. And right now, she's mad at her brother, and that makes it twice as bad."

"But she's not mad at you, is she?" she asked softly, walking toward the exit with him.

"No," he answered with a twinkle in his eye. "She's not mad at me. She loves me . . . and I love her, so what could be wrong?"

"*Exactly,*" she agreed, and her heart gave a painful lurch. "You've got each other."

Tom filled her in on the upcoming session as he threaded his way along the highways back into the city. Crissy was once again surprised when she saw the traffic. It never seemed to slow down in New York. "We're going to need a talking baby bear and a little boy for this one," he told her. "And how do you think you might do as *Mrs.* Santa Claus?" he asked, then chuckled.

"Mrs. Santa Claus?" she repeated. "Oh, I forgot this is another rush job for the Christmas sales season."

"Can you believe we've already bought the time to begin the promotion next week?"

"Whew!" She whistled. "That's really cutting it close. I can see I'll be up most of the night doing the preliminary construction of the voices."

"Well, it wouldn't have been such a rush if you'd agreed sooner to do it," he shot back, showing just how tired and strained he was feeling.

"Or if James hadn't been so damn pigheaded about insisting on only me—her—oh, damn!"

Tom laughed self-consciously. "I'm sorry, Belle. I apologize. You just can't imagine what it's like to be under the gun on a twenty-four-hour basis, no matter where he is," he explained, suggesting that James could be a tyrant when he was angry.

"I have some idea." She seethed, still angry herself. She did not see the quizzical look Tom gave her.

Within the hour, Crissy had been escorted to her room at the Hilton. She told Tom she would take a cab to the office and arrive at 8:30. Then she hung up her tailored black dress and quickly showered and changed into her robe, curling up comfortably on her bed to begin studying the script. One of the most difficult voices would be that of the little boy, expressing breathless delight over his handsome wooden Christmas toys. Again and again, she experimented, using her tape recorder, which she was thankful to have remembered to stick into her suitcase at the last moment.

By 3:00 A.M., she felt she had mastered all three—the talking baby bear, the little boy, and Mrs. Santa Claus. She was happy as she munched the remains of her ham and cheese on rye, sent up by room service, and listened to her recorded voice.

"Santa Claus only chooses the best, my dears," she was saying. "And the best toys are Prince toys!" And the best man is Mr. Prince, that she could not deny.

She forced herself to rest, knowing deep sleep was the only thing that would carry her through the next day. She was determined to do the best job she had ever done with this commercial, and her voice had to be fine-tuned for the assignment.

Her wake-up call came at seven. She stretched sleepily and slipped from beneath the warm covers, padding into the connecting bath to look at her face. Yes, she was rested, that she could see. Her face had lost some of the signs of the strain of recent events, and her body felt strong again. After she bathed and carefully applied her sophisticated makeup, she put on her silk teddy, sighing as the smooth garment hugged her flesh. Then she stepped into her pencil-slim, lined black wool dress and adjusted the deep neckline and the fitted long sleeves, closing the tiny zippers at her wrists and the one at her back.

Her ruby tulip necklace winked back at her in the dressing-table mirror. She touched the charm lovingly, knowing today she was doing the last good thing she could ever do for James. She hoped in this small way to return to him some measure of the love she had so unwisely lost. Shuddering against the loneliness she knew would follow her for the rest of her life, she touched a clear red gloss to her full, sensuous lips, then brushed her hair until it sparkled in shining ebony curls.

She placed a close-fitting black silk hat at an angle over her eyes. The narrow brim supported a medium-weave veil with tiny black dots woven into the net. She pulled it down over her beautiful oval face. Finally, she slipped her black-stockinged feet into extremely high heels—open-toe black pumps, which were the latest fashion—and hooked her black fox wrap around her narrow shoulders. After an understated mist of heady Taboo perfume, she was ready.

She stepped back from the mirror to take in her entire length. She smiled mysteriously. She might not feel like a million, she mused sadly, but she certainly looked like a million. And in New York City, that said it all! Picking up her slim black leather clutch bag, she dropped the key inside and walked serenely out the door. It was time for her greatest performance, and she prayed she was ready for the challenge.

When her cab pulled up to the skyscraper where J-R Advertising was located, she paid the driver, tipping him handsomely, and as she stepped from the taxi, she found herself looking furtively around her. Some instinct warned her that James was near. That wasn't possible, she told herself scoffingly. Tom had given her his word. Driving her paranoid feelings from her mind, she entered the building and was soon being lifted with great speed to the forty-second floor and her secret assignment.

Tom was waiting for her when the elevator doors slid open. "Good morning, beautiful lady." He beamed. "Or should I say, 'beautiful, *sophisticated* lady,' for you surely are that. It's difficult to believe you're the same woman I picked up at the airport at midnight. Does it have something to do with the witching hour, Belle?" he asked, still chuckling warmly.

"No, *dahling,*" she answered theatrically. "It only means I know I'm in New York City."

"Let's do it—what do you say?"

She nodded and took his proffered arm, suddenly feeling in need of some support. Inside the agency, the receptionist greeted her with a cheery, "Good morning." Crissy returned the greeting and continued to the recording studio, where Tom introduced her to the producer, director, and editor of the commercial. Their faces were new to her, but she swallowed any shyness she might have felt and shook each one's hand in turn, using her best professional manners because she was eager for the session to go smoothly.

If she could make everyone feel at ease, then her nerves would settle down too. And the job would go quickly. Already she longed for her God-made mountains, feeling closed in and trapped among the man-made stone and steel structures of this metropolis. She removed her fox wrap and hat, and kicked off her shoes to signal that she was ready to begin. The four, including Tom, laughed at her antics, and she knew the ice was broken. Everything would go well.

Early on, Tom was called away for a business call, but Crissy was hardly aware of his disappearance. She was totally immersed in her project; nothing short of an earthquake would break her concentration now. She found her three co-workers to be among the most cooperative people with whom she had worked in her five years of doing commercial voices. They shared ideas, listened attentively to hers, and were never short-tempered or churlish in their instructions. But it was an extremely long session, lasting well into the afternoon. They had stopped for short breaks so Crissy could rest her vocal chords, but for the most part it was a straight-through session that ended, finally, at four. She was exhausted when Tom came in to see how things were going.

"It's all wrapped up." She sighed happily. "I only hope your client finds the tapes satisfactory," she added, feeling let down by more than just having finished the project. "I'm going back home, Tom. Want to walk me to the elevator?" She replaced her hat and slipped back into her stylish shoes. She smiled her thanks when he helped her with her wrap. "I'm going back to my mountains, away from the madding crowds." She was only half jesting.

Tom gave his slim gold watch a furtive glance, and drawled, "Ah, what's your hurry, Belle? Let's go into my office for a short visit before you leave. God knows when we'll see each other again. This business is so erratic, you never can tell what's going to happen in the next minute. And you must be famished," he added. "I'll have a sandwich sent up from the deli downstairs. What do you say?"

"Thanks for the offer, Tom," she said, smiling beautifully because she felt she had done her best work ever, and even if she hadn't received payment, this job had been done for love. For love of James, the only man who had ever breached her defenses against involvement. But now it was time to steal away home. Time for the long process of healing her broken heart. "I've really got to fly—no pun intended." She laughed softly, bringing sparkling lights of gold into her wide brown eyes. "Some instinct is telling me I have to go . . . *now*, or I'm going to regret it. I know it's unreasonable, but that's just the way it is. The hair on the back of my neck is standing on end. And it has something to do with James." A bittersweet smile came to her lips and she turned toward the hall.

"I wish you would stay, Belle," he entreated, looking uncomfortable and tugging at his dark silk tie. She narrowed her eyes suspiciously; Tom caught her penetrating glance and averted his eyes, looking at the wall clock, which showed 4:30. "But if you gotta go, you gotta go," he said nervously. He guided her to the elevator and kissed her lightly through the veil on her cheek. "That's a sexy hat, lady," he remarked with a growl, squeezing her hand in a final good-bye. "See ya, honey," he called as the door enclosed her slim well-dressed form.

"See ya," she murmured, feeling tears threaten to blind her vision. Her stomach fluttered as the elevator carried her swiftly to the lobby. Her chin held high, she walked straight toward the exit, eager to flag down a cab to take her back to her hotel so she could change and catch the next flight home. She had only taken a dozen steps when she caught the unmistakable, erect outline of James as he strode forward, heading right toward her.

Her steps faltered momentarily, then she hurriedly decided he would never recognize her in the high-fashion ensemble and veiled hat. Still staring at the door beyond, forcing herself not to break into a run, she passed within three feet of him. She was just getting ready to take her first full breath after the threatened encounter when she felt a hand fall lightly on her arm and heard his deep, familiar voice. What was she going to do now? she thought, frantically searching her mind for a means of escape.

"I beg your pardon, miss," he began, his words vibrating to her very soul. "I couldn't help noticing your unusual necklace, and I wondered if you'd tell me where you got it. It's very becom—" He stopped in mid-sentence and stared through the veil at Crissy's wide eyes. "My God! Crissy, it's *you*. What are you doing in New York?" he demanded, his grip slowly tightening on her wrist as if he were afraid she might disappear before his eyes.

She sent a prayer heavenward and was immediately rewarded for her faith. Another lie, she lamented, and after so many. "Hello, James," she said calmly, ordering her heart to still its hammering and her knees to cease their quaking. "I'm just in town for a few days," she explained confidently, sure she was going to bring it off. "I'm attending a class reunion at NYC and visiting some old friends while I'm here." She smiled serenely and looked James squarely in the eye. She was surprised to see how drawn and haggard he looked. But he would be feeling better very soon, she thought, her heart melting at his touch. "I'm surprised that you've come back to the city so soon. As I remember, you were just here," she said smoothly, thankful for all her years of training.

His hand remained linked around her wrist, and Crissy knew she wasn't going anyplace until he decided to release her. "I left home again this morning after I spoke with Tom. He finally got Belle Grady's consent to do our project, and I'm on my way upstairs now to meet her. She's not quite finished with her taping, I suspect, but I was determined to meet her personally. I wanted to thank her for her help. She was the only one I ever wanted," he added, unaware of his own double meaning.

"The Prince wins again," she teased softly. "I'm truly glad Mr. Sinclair was able to convince her. Especially since you believed she was the only one for the job," she said sincerely. "Now, if you'll excuse me, I have an appointment with friends. Good-bye, James. It was lovely seeing you again," she told him, gently trying to disengage her arm from his hold.

"Don't go just yet, Crissy," he said suddenly. "I owe you an apology after the way I cut you off on the phone the other night. My damnable pride got in the way of my good sense," he muttered gruffly. "And I've been kicking myself ever since." His hold tightened again, and his voice broke with emotion. "I've missed you, baby. Can you forgive me?"

Her heart swelled with the realization of the effort it took James to apologize. He had swallowed his wounded pride to say those words. But she was still uneasy about a future they might share, so she only replied, "Apology accepted."

He winced at his echoed words. Had he lost her forever? No, dammit, he refused to accept defeat. He was going to marry this stubborn woman if he had to go to hell and back to make it happen. And right now, he wasn't going to let her out of his sight!

"I want you to meet Belle and to listen to the new commercial. The editor was going to do the sound mix as soon as they finished the session." He was already guiding her back to the same elevator that had brought her down.

Frantically she groped for any believable reason to get away from him. "I can't, James," she insisted, feeling hysteria beginning to take over her usually intelligent brain. "I haven't the time."

He smiled down into her wide eyes, now ablaze with disquieting fear . . . of him . . . and of what he might find out in her presence.

"Surely you can spare a few minutes from your busy schedule to come with me," he suggested, dropping his voice to a low whisper. "Do it as a favor for me, Crissy. For old times' sake," he requested cryptically, already pushing the button to close the elevator doors.

Resignedly, she silently nodded in assent as the elevator rose.

"That's my mountain gal," he murmured enthusiastically. "I must admit, though, you look more like a Paris model in that little number." He gazed appreciately from her veil-covered face to her black-stockinged toes and back again, dwelling for an instant on her necklace, lying warm against her rounded breasts. "It's the sort of outfit that makes a man wonder what's underneath," he said just as the door slid open to the agency.

She pulled back into a corner of the elevator, saying hoarsely, "I've changed my mind, James. I'll leave you here." She reached for the button for the lobby, but James was too quick for her. He placed his fingers around her slim wrist and literally plucked her from the box a moment before the doors slid shut again. Her face was flushed with outrage now, and, she had to admit, from his closeness. Just who did he think he was, manhandling her?

He was quick to see her rising temper, and just as quickly extinguished it with his next words. "Stay with me, Crissy. Please?" he murmured, close to her ear, making Crissy feel as if she'd follow the Prince to the ends of the earth.

Defeated, she shrugged in acquiescence and walked by his side into the reception area. At once she was on guard against any slip of the agency's personnel as to her identity. The receptionist looked up with surprise, then smiled, saying, "Why, hello, Mr. Prince. It's very nice to see you again so soon." Turning to Crissy, the woman was about to say the same thing to Belle Grady, but a secretive signal from Crissy's menacing eyes reminded the woman of her strict orders about Belle. "Hello, Miss . . .?"

James introduced her, putting a casual arm around her waist. "Sharon, I'd like you to meet Crissy Brant. Ms. Brant is a friend of mine from Missouri," he explained easily. "We're here to see Tom."

"Good afternoon, Ms. Brant," responded the woman. "It's a pleasure meeting you." Crissy watched as Sharon glanced back and forth between her and James, her mind doing calisthenics, trying to figure out this new information. "I'll tell Mr. Sinclair you're on your way, Mr. Prince."

James smiled his thanks and gently pushed Crissy forward, down the hall. Tom was standing at his door, waiting for them. Crissy surreptitiously examined his expression and decided he looked like a cat who had just swallowed the canary—and it was an imported bird! She remembered how he had tried to keep her in his office a few moments ago, then just as quickly had rescinded his invitation after he glanced at the clock. If he set me up, I'll kill him. She was seething and wanted to scream at the top of her lungs.

Tom, however, paid no attention to her glare. Instead, he thrust his hand out heartily to shake James's. "James, glad you could make it. I think you're going to be very pleased with the end results of our collective efforts. It looks like you've got an award-winning commercial on your hands. It also looks like you're going to sell a whole lot of toys," he said emphatically. "I hope you're prepared." Then he turned to Crissy with a quizzical look in his eyes. "I don't believe we've met."

"Tom, I'd like you to meet Crissy Brant," James said crisply. "Crissy, this is Tom Sinclair. I believe you both know a little about each other," he added in a flat voice.

Crissy forced herself to smile kindly at Tom and extended her hand to him. "Mr. Sinclair. It's a pleasure meeting you. I understand your fiancée is James's sister . . . Julie, isn't it?"

"Ms. Brant, the pleasure is all mine, I assure you, and yes, my wife-to-be is Julie, James's sister," he replied. "She's just as lovely as you, beautiful lady," he said smoothly, still holding her hand, "but in a different way. She has James's coloring. Golden hair and olive skin . . . but she *doesn't* have that great hairy moustache." He laughed heartily. "Thank God!"

Crissy could hardly repress the giggle that bubbled to her lips. James looked as if he wanted to sock his future brother-in-law. She hadn't realized how touchy he was about his looks . . . or could he be jealous? Was it remotely possible?

James cleared his throat and glared openly at Tom and then at Crissy, and the giggle escaped her. She tried to cover her laugh with a cough, but it was obvious that James saw right through her little smokescreen. "Shall we get on with it?" he muttered, shooting furious visual messages at Tom.

Tom swallowed nervously. "I have one bit of unpleasant news for you, James," he informed him cautiously. "Ah . . . Belle Grady had another commitment and she couldn't stay to meet you. She wanted to, believe me," he hastened to add. "But it just wasn't possible, given her busy schedule."

James filled the air with a soft string of salty expletives. "I'll be damned!" he exclaimed. "She's a damn ghost, that's what she is. Are you absolutely certain she even exists?" he asked Tom.

"Oh, she's real, all right, James," came the answer. Tom threw a teasing look at Crissy, who was bridling. "Maybe she just likes her privacy."

"Like someone else I know," James muttered, glaring directly at Crissy. "Come on. Let's get this over with," he ordered, leading the way toward the sound room.

Crissy dragged along behind him, feeling as if she were walking the last few steps to her own execution, but then she overheard Tom's hurried command to the others over the intercom. "*Watch it!* The Prince is on his way . . . with Belle, but he doesn't know it, so mum's the word." And she felt her heart begin to beat once more.

James insisted on introducing her all around, and eventually they sat down to hear the tape. He listened with his eyes closed, seemingly savoring every syllable of the script. Crissy watched him as his mouth curved into a satisfied smile when he heard her voice as, first, the baby bear, and then the little laughing child. "Isn't she great?" he enthused softly, his smile broadening when he listened to her as Mrs. Santa Claus.

Crissy had not taken the time to wait for the completed mix, so she sat up in surprise when she heard Santa Claus's voice come throbbing from the speaker. James opened his eyes to meet her questioning gaze. He nodded his head in affirmation. "I've done some commercials before, and it saved me from paying someone else. Belle's work costs an arm and a leg . . . but she's worth every penny," he stated emphatically. "Every penny!"

The commercial came to a close, but a few seconds before the end, Crissy was startled to hear the mating call of the cardinal. This time when she looked at James, his face was slightly flushed, and he wore a rather sheepish expression. He shrugged his shoulders nonchalantly and whispered, "So I like redbirds!"

Her pulse began to race with hope. Was there a chance he had decided to forgive her after all? Could she still have her impossible dream? A few measures of "Jingle Bells" completed the tape, and then everyone was speaking at once. It was a foregone conclusion that this commercial was going to do great things for Prince Toys.

Excitedly, the editor came out of the control room, beaming with pleasure. "I think it's the best work we've ever done," he declared, enthusiastically. "Belle, you were just—"

Each person in the room froze. The deadly silence ricocheted off the walls. A mumbled, "Oh, my God!" wheezed from the editor's pale lips, and he looked as if he would have been happy to die at that very moment.

Slowly James turned to face Crissy, who wished she had the courage to throw herself out the forty-second-story window. His glare pinned her to the spot. *"You're Belle Grady?"* he asked incredulously, his voice threaded with steel.

She could only nod. Then suddenly everyone was talking once again.

"Tom, why in the hell didn't you *tell* me?" roared James.

"Tom, you *promised* you wouldn't let James know until I was out of the city," accused Crissy.

"I'm sorry as I can be," croaked the embarrassed editor.

Tom put his fingers between his teeth and let loose an ear-splitting whistle. Instantly the room was still. Calmly he took charge of the chaotic scene. "Now, then. One question at a time, *please,*" he entreated. "First, James, I couldn't tell you because I gave Belle—Crissy—my word. Crissy, I had to tell James you were doing the session today because this morning he fired me for not getting you to record! Ed, don't be upset about the slip," he told the editor reassuringly. "Hell, you were just so happy, you forgot, that's all."

Turning back to James and Crissy, he confirmed her last hunch. "And yes, Crissy, before you even ask, I did double duty today. I was busy playing Cupid all afternoon, trying to keep you here, and hoping—fervently hoping," he said to James, "that you could get here before she left. I figured if I could get you two stubborn people to talk, you might realize you love each other, and let me get some work done for a change," he stated bravely, not sure if he would be fired again on the spot.

"How could James fire you, Tom?" she exclaimed. "He's not your boss anymore."

This time James took the reins. "Oh, yes, I am, Crissy—at least for the time being," he added, eyeing Tom threateningly. "I still hold the controlling interest in this agency," he explained, a vengeful look lighting his stormy blue eyes.

"Would you like to step into my office?" Tom suggested, obviously relieved that the scene had not cost him his job.

"No," replied James in the same steely voice. "We'll be at my apartment. Don't call!" he ordered pointedly. Then he grabbed Crissy around the waist and began striding toward the exit.

"Where do you think you're dragging me, you big gorilla?" She tried feverishly to pull away, but got nowhere. "You can't do this. This is kidnapping. James! *James!*"

Ten

The elevator opened as if upon the Prince's command, and James pushed Crissy, none too gently, inside. He turned to her and commanded, "Just shut up, Crissy! Don't say another word! I'm teetering on the edge of violence, and one more word out of you may push me over. Either be still or take the consequences. I'm not responsible for my actions at this moment," he added threateningly, thrusting his fists into his trouser pockets.

Crissy knew he meant every word, and cowered in the corner. When they reached the lobby, he pulled her arm through his and strode grimly toward the exit. Crissy tried to remove her hand, complaining, "James, I can't walk this fast. Stop dragging me!"

Although he did shorten his angry strides to better match her step, the way he glared into her frightened brown eyes told her he was making the concession against his better judgment. "That's rich!" he snarled, laughing harshly. "Especially from a woman who makes a habit of running away," he barked. Without another word, he shoved her into the revolving door, making sure his tall, taut length was jammed into the same compartment.

"Don't even think it," he ordered menacingly, noting her frantic search for a taxi.

As if by magic, as soon as James brought her to the curb, a cab appeared. In seconds he bundled her into the back seat, slammed the door hard, and directed the cabbie. "Park Avenue . . . the Euclid Manor," he ordered, throwing his arm around Crissy and holding her in a paralyzing grip.

Crissy was over her first fright now, and she felt anger begin to rip through her body. "I am *not* going to your apartment, James," she said, raising her voice in fury. "I'm going *home*. Driver, take me to the Hilton Hotel . . . at once."

"You're coming with me," he snapped, holding on to her fighting body as if she were a child having a tantrum.

"No, *no!*" she shouted. "Driver, the Hilton."

"Which'll it be, buddy?" the driver asked calmly, directing his question to James.

"Park Avenue, where else?" he countered. "What we have here is a hysterical midwesterner, Mac," he explained, matching his tone of voice with the New York vernacular. "The traffic is driving her bananas," he explained over the din of the blaring horns. "As soon as I get her home, I'll take care of her," he told him, sounding apologetic, but his words conveyed a threat to Crissy.

The cabbie nodded in understanding. "Consider it done, buddy," he promised, and cut across the busy street with daredevil skill. "Outsiders just ain't up to it."

Crissy opened her mouth to voice her contempt for both men, but James's grip on her shoulder became bonecrushing. "Just can the chatter, sister," he said bitingly, but his hooded eyes hid the sparks of humor that were dancing there.

"*Can the chatter . . . sister?*" she repeated in disbelief, rolling her eyes in a wide heavenward arc. "Oh, this is too much!" She jerked her body, still trying to break his iron hold.

Menacingly he leaned over to speak into Crissy's ear. His words reverberated inside her brain. "You're on my turf now, baby . . . and you haven't got a chance!" She sat as straight and stiff as she was able under the circumstances, and glared, unspeaking, out the side window for the rest of the terrifying ride.

In a short time the cabbie pulled up, brakes screeching, to the Euclid Manor. James gave him a large bill and his thanks. "You're a man of the world, Mac. Thanks!"

"Thank *you*," the driver replied. "Jeez, after driving a hack for twenty years, there ain't much I ain't seen," he answered philosophically. He sliced a glance along the slim length of Crissy's figure when the pair got out, his eyes lighting with pleasure. "I wish you luck, buddy, she looks like she's worth savin'." He chuckled knowingly.

"*That* remains to be seen, Mac," James retorted darkly, exchanging a worldly salute with the driver before he spun Crissy around and headed her toward the canapy-protected entrance. "Johnson," he greeted the uniformed doorman, giving him a brisk nod, and sweeping Crissy into the lobby and the waiting elevator. Silently he jabbed the penthouse button and the couple rose to the top floor. "Come on," he ordered, dragging her across the hall to the massive door. Quickly he withdrew a key from his pocket and jammed it into the lock, giving the door a hefty shove when it opened. "Inside," he ordered again, locking the door behind him.

Crissy stood to her full height, trying as best she could to show James she wasn't the least bit intimidated by his caveman tactics. Her show of strength was completely wasted, because he left her standing there to face her inner fear alone. Her bewildered eyes were able to observe the decor of the lush apartment. It was done in the same brown tones as his lake home.

James had disappeared into the living room. She could hear bottles and glasses clinking noisily and assumed he was pouring himself a stiff drink. She couldn't hide the smile that curved her full mouth. I've driven him to drink, she mused. A tiny shiver of triumph raised her sagging spirits. *Serves him right!* After all, he did the same thing to me!

Some of the fear and anger drained from her body as she stood there. The fashionable splendor of the room beyond was in her line of vision. A long, modern beige couch faced a massive fireplace. It was balanced by two rounded, cocoa velvet chairs. The darker beige carpeting looked thick and expensive, and the mellow wood tables were antiques. Exquisite small sculpted pieces were arranged upon the mantel and some of the tables. It was a beautiful room, Crissy decided, but her eyes were drawn again and again to the bold, vibrant painting that hung above the fireplace. Red tulips! The modern graphic design was balanced by a heavy, ornately carved gold frame.

As her eyes fastened on the fiery color of the canvas, her heart tripped over itself. Maybe, just maybe, she still had a chance. At that moment James came around the corner of the arch and stood staring at her.

"Well, are you going to stand there all day?" he wondered aloud, his voice softening when she refused to meet his eyes. He walked casually over to stand in front of her and nonchalantly took her black fox fur from her shoulders. Her eyes snapped at his assumption that she would stay, but she refused to get into another shouting match with him. He smiled then, for the first time since he had discovered her secret identity. "Please come inside, Crissy," he cajoled softly. "You have some explaining to do," he added, his tone of voice contradicting his threatening words.

Finally Crissy found her tongue, and lashed out at him. "I don't have to explain a damn thing to you,

James," she retorted angrily, but her heart's vision was extremely impressed with his calm stature as he stood before her, looking urbane and handsome in his dark gray pin-striped business suit and burgundy silk tie. "You don't own me, you know!" she argued defiantly.

"No," he agreed smoothly, guiding her nonetheless into the sumptuous room. "But you *could* use a keeper," he suggested.

She jerked from his hold and faced him squarely. "I didn't have a bit of trouble until you came into my life," she yelled.

"And you didn't have much of a life either," he shot back heartlessly, hitting her vulnerable spot with expert marksmanship. He watched in silent surprise as Crissy's face crumpled before his menacing gaze. Great tears of distress gathered at the corners of her wide, alarmed eyes and began to trickle down her cheeks beneath the veil of her sophisticated little black hat.

She began to sniffle loudly, her shoulders trembling from unhappiness. "Oh, James," she whimpered. "Why do we have to fight all the time? I don't want to fight anymore," she cried, sobbing openly now.

In an instant James had pulled her into his crushing embrace. "Crissy, darling," he agreed with a husky sigh. "I don't want to fight you either. All I ever wanted to do was love you, baby," he explained softly, holding her close to his strong body until, trying to stop crying, she took a deep, shuddering breath to regain control of her emotions. Tenderly he lifted the veil from her tear-streaked face and removed her hat, setting it precariously on the end table at his knee. "That's a sexy little hat. Is it new?" he asked, in an effort to make Crissy feel relaxed.

She stood very still as he carefully blotted her tears with his handkerchief, and replied, whimpering, "I got it at a little boutique on Fifth Avenue the last time I was in town." She took the white linen from his fingers and blew her nose, unceremoniously handing it back to him when she was through. He slipped the damp square into his jacket pocket and continued to hold her.

"Feeling better now?" he asked, solicitously. She nodded. Quietly he stood away from her and slid out of his jacket, throwing it over the chair. Then, loosening his tie and unfastening the first two buttons of his shirt with one hand, he took her hand with the other and led her to the couch. Without a word, he sank down into its soft cushions and pulled her gently onto his lap. She snuggled within his embrace, burying her face against his neck. "Now, Crissy, talk to me," he murmured into her soft curls. "Begin at the beginning and don't leave out anything," he ordered quietly.

She took a great gulp of breath, knowing the time had arrived when she had to prove her trust in James, when she had to take the chance that he could still love her, and would not hurt her. "I've always kept my commercial career a secret," she began in a trembling voice. "No one knew about it—none of my friends or peers—only the few people with whom I worked at the agencies. And *they* never knew exactly where I lived . . . they only had the unlisted phone numbers where I could be reached. Those people, Tom among them, were sworn to secrecy. I made it plain that I would refuse any future contracts with them if they broke their word. Five years ago I had a very bad experience with a man I thought I could trust. Also, I hated the thought of being hounded by some of those gossipy, publicity-seeking reporters," she explained softly. "I was determined to live my life the way I wanted to, and without publicity. I didn't need it. I was as busy as I wanted to be. And with my teaching and summer work, I was very satisfied with my life." She sighed again, and moved closer in his arms.

"Of course, you know you could never have had the agencies' promise if you weren't the best in the business, don't you?" he asked tenderly. "You *are* the best." He spoke so warmly that, for a moment, Crissy wondered if he was still talking about her professional skills.

"And why didn't you think you could let me share your secret, honey?"

She tried to make herself small in James's arms, feeling uncertain now that she was facing the moment of truth. "I was afraid," she whispered. "I didn't know if you really loved me."

"Don't you mean you didn't know if you could trust me?" he countered, prodding her gently. "Crissy?"

Tentatively she lifted her free arm, letting her fingers creep around his neck, pulling him closer as she replied, her warm breath whispering the words against his throat. "Isn't it all the same thing?" she asked timidly. She drew away so she could see his face, and was surprised to see that his features had taken on a serene glow. His eyes were closed, and he took such deep breaths that it seemed as if he hadn't been breathing at all for the last few seconds.

Then he opened his eyes and she looked into their deep blue depths, feeling herself get weak all over. "So . . ." He sighed, his smile warming her blood. "You've finally realized that love and trust are one and the same," he declared, relieved. "But why, after all these days, have you decided to tell me all your secrets?" he wanted to know, still determined to hear it all.

She gulped audibly. A look of fear shadowed her dark eyes. He was asking for everything now. Could she tell him? Could she make the final trusting commitment? His eyes locked with hers, and the warm glow of his gaze gave her the strength. "I'm taking the biggest chance of my life, James," she began. "I'm trusting you with this secret because I want you. There's no other man in the world for me." She took another deep breath and plunged headlong into the center of her hopes and dreams. "I love you," she whispered in a trembling voice. "I love *you!*"

Crissy continued to look into James's eyes. He did not speak. He just looked at her with startling intensity. As Crissy watched, she saw tears gather in his blue eyes. And she returned his tremulous smile with one of her own. Her heart rejoiced. It was going to be all right. He loved her still!

Slowly he bent his head and kissed her with a sweetness so glorious she thought her heart would burst with gratitude and joy. When he lifted his gentle lips from hers, he finally responded. "Do you have any idea how happy you've just made me, darling? I've loved you from the first moment I set eyes on you, with your crazy tulip hat and gamin smile," he told her huskily. "I'd been searching for my mate all my life, and when I found you, I couldn't believe my good fortune. And I thought I might have been just a little bit crazy, too. *Imagine* . . . falling in love with a mountain gal . . . who wears *clodhoppers*!" He grimaced, chuckling happily. "I always pictured the girl of my dreams as a fashion plate," he went on, hurrying to qualify his explanation. "And look at you—I have a fashionable woman and a carefree child all rolled into one beautiful package." He kissed her again.

"Not a child," she grumbled good-naturedly.

"No," he agreed at once. "Not a child, but a woman with childlike qualities," he murmured, melting her bones with his ardent gaze and setting her flesh on fire with his touch. "A woman I'm going to spend the rest of my life touching and adoring and showing how much I love her," he promised, kissing her with a ferocity that took Crissy's breath away.

"I was afraid I'd lost you," she admitted. "I was so hurt when I apologized and you accepted it in such a cold way. I thought you hated me." She sighed, trembling at the mere thought.

"I never hated you, sweetheart," he said, holding her close. "But I'm a street fighter . . . always have been. And street fighters learn early that sometimes they have to protect their backsides against a threatening situation. I didn't think you would ever grow to trust me, Crissy, so the natural thing for me to do was to put my back against the wall and fight you. It was self-preservation, that's all. And I'm sorry I hurt you in the process, baby. Will you forgive me?" he pleaded, his love for her warming his words.

"Yes," she breathed. "I know now how much I hurt you too. Just don't ever leave me, darling."

"Not a chance," he retorted gruffly. "You're stuck with me now, babe."

Suddenly he leaped up from the couch, careful not to let her fall, setting her gingerly on her feet. "We'll be married this week at the little chapel in Silver Dollar City," he exclaimed, smiling broadly, his eyes telling her how his mind was ticking off details. "The park is closed now, so we'll have the whole place to ourselves. I always thought that little church was a slice of heaven, with its huge picture window behind the pulpit looking out over miles and miles of Ozark mountains and valleys," he enthused. "Will that please you, sweetheart?" he asked, unnecessarily, because Crissy had already clapped her hands with delight at his beautiful idea. He hugged her tightly and swung her around in his arms. "I *found* you there. I want to *marry* you there."

Straightening, he peered into her radiant face. "My God, in all the excitement I forgot to propose. Darling Crissy, will you marry me and spend the rest of your life sharing our love?" His eyes revealed the depths of his feelings for her.

In reply she stood on tiptoe and kissed him. The kiss held all the love she felt for this unorthodox, wonderful man she held in her arms. He groaned uncontrollably, moving his hands along her spine, finally settling at her hips to pull her hard against his shuddering body. When the kiss ended, he was breathing raggedly, but found the strength to ask teasingly, "Was that a yes or a maybe?"

"That, my darling, was an unqualified yes!"

"No doubts? No hidden worries?" he insisted.

"None!" she said seriously. "I trust you, James."

"Ahhh, baby, those are the sweetest words this man ever hopes to hear," he mumbled happily. Then he returned to their wedding plans. "We'll have to call

all your relatives, Crissy. Billy and Johnny must come with little Crissy, Jr. Does she look like you?" he asked, not waiting for her reply as he rushed on. "And Granny? Will she come out of the hills for your wedding? Of course she will . . . she loves you as much as I do! Then we'll have to make arrangements for Julie and Tom to fly in," he went on. "They can stay at the lake house." He laughed heartily. "Wouldn't it be terrific if Tom could convince Julie to marry him while they're in the Ozarks? That man has his work cut out for him. My sister is a stubborn soul," he declared, winking broadly at Crissy in order to drive home the point that he also was going to have a time with her.

His blue eyes narrowed suspiciously as she stood silently. "Cris-sy? There's something more you haven't told me, isn't there?" he asked pointedly. "Well, I'm waiting!" His voice was menacing and as he folded his arms across his chest and spread his legs apart, he looked very powerful.

Crissy stumbled away from him and walked over to the fireplace, clutching the mantel with nerveless fingers, trying to find the strength to make her last confession. He watched her with glinting eyes, stalking her every move. Finally she took a deep breath and lifted her downcast, thick lashes to meet his penetrating gaze. He was just standing there by the couch, his hands now balled into fists on his lean hips . . . waiting!

"Y-y-you know I l-love you with all my h-heart," she stuttered. "Y-you b-believe that, don't y-you?"

"Yes, *yes,*" he said with a growl, his look pinning her to the spot. "Get on with it, Crissy," he ordered grimly, bracing himself for yet another surprise.

"We-e-ll," she began again, smiling tremulously. "I have a few messages for you," she told him. He nodded with a jerk, not able to speak another word until he knew what the hell she was talking about. "Here are the messages," she began, explaining absolutely nothing . . . yet!

"Pul-ease, *pul-ease*, love Crissy," she begged in her answering-service voice.

"Crissy loves you, I'm *sure*," she gushed in Billy's style, punctuating her words with a girlish giggle. "And my Johnny and Crissy Junior think so, too," she added.

"Crissy's got a powerful love fer ya, Jimmy Bob," exclaimed Tulip.

And, finally, she became Granny's crackly, wizened voice. "My Crystabelle's old enuf to know her own mind, young feller. She sez she loves ya, Jimmy. And I reckon you loves her back, cuz you done admitted she can ring yore chimes." She cackled, then laughed raucously.

The look of incredulity and shock that had replaced James's angry scowl made Crissy cringe. She had no idea how he was going to take this. After all, he was a man who would not appreciate being made the fool. She held her breath as she waited.

In slow motion James began to shake his head, his face still showing his surprise at this unexpected turn of events. "Well, I'll be damned," he said, his voice filled with wonder. "I'll be damned," he said again. He began to snicker, still shaking his head in disbelief. Finally the force of his laughter broke through, and he filled the room with hearty chuckles and outright guffaws, releasing his delight to the world. Once started, he could not seem to control his reaction, and he fell weakly upon the long couch, holding his sides and howling.

Her little recital seemed to have snapped something inside him, and Crissy ran to kneel at his side, crying out tearfully, "James! *James!* Can you ever forgive me?"

"Forgive you?" he gasped between laughs he was trying to control. "I'm absolutely *outraged*!" he roared, breaking into another deafening peal of laughter.

When he could speak coherently again, he said breathlessly, "No one, but *no one* has ever put one over on me." He crowed, still finding it almost impossible to stop his howls. "I fell for your little act, hook, line, and sinker. Man, you'll never let me live this one down, will you?" The tears were still running down his flushed face. "I can hardly wait till April Fool's Day." He groaned, holding his stomach against the pain.

"But *do* you forgive me?" she cried, beside herself now.

"It *was* a very dirty trick, Crissy," he insisted, trying heroically to look the part of the injured party, but his hand was stealing along her back and settled on her firm bottom.

She smoothed his hair from his brow and caressed his face tenderly. "I know. I know," she admitted, mournfully. "But I was only trying to find out what you really felt for me," she explained softly.

"So you'd know if you could trust me?" he questioned, continuing his erotic stroking of her body, knowing his hands were sending a totally different message to her flesh than his words.

She began to cover his face with tiny butterfly kisses, hoping he could understand that her playacting was not necessary now. "That was before I knew for sure that you loved me, James," she whispered. "You have to admit, it's very funny now."

He rolled effortlessly to his feet and pulled her up beside him. "Oh, yes, Crissy. It's one of the funniest things that has ever happened to me," he replied. "Now, then, how shall I answer your request for forgiveness?" he wondered aloud, casually finding and unzipping the wrist closings on her understated, slim black dress.

"Let's see, now." He pondered as if considering an earth-shattering decision. He put his hands gently on her soft shoulders and kissed her chastely on the forehead. "*That* is for little Crissy, Junior." He lowered his head slightly and planted a moist little kiss on the tip of her nose. "And *that* is for Billy and her Johnny." When he kissed her right cheek, he told her it was for her answering service, and when he kissed her left cheek with more warmth, he murmured, "That one is for your granny. I really wish I might have met that woman."

Crissy had become a melding figure of desire as he forgave all of her characters their sins of commission. She sighed softly, and smiled in rapture as she felt his experienced fingers seek and find the back zipper of her dress and steadily pull the fastener down below her waist. "You know, Crissy, my love, it's a good thing I gave you the ruby tulip necklace," he admonished. "Me thinks you were in such a jangle this morning—giving me what you knew I wanted—that you forgot to add your personal red trademark," he murmured, slowly pushing her dress from her shoulders and watching as it fell around her feet on the thick carpet.

When his eyes returned to her voluptuous figure, he sucked in his breath in masculine pleasure. She gave him her most radiant smile, reading his reaction correctly as his smoldering gaze drank in her beautiful curves, clad only in her red silk teddy. "Well, I'll be damned," he croaked. "Fooled again . . . three times in one day!" he exclaimed softly, molding her thrusting breasts with his warm hands, feeling the peaks harden instantaneously under his hot touch.

She chuckled throatily at his consternation. "But I love you . . . *forever*, James," she purred, coming into his arms, feeling his hands begin their feverish exploration of her body.

"And I love you," he breathed softly against her throat as he continued to kiss her with rising passion. "You're my life," he whispered, sweeping her high into his arms and turning toward the hall leading to his bedroom. He walked steadily toward the open door, carrying her in his arms as if she were the most precious possession a man could ever hold. Stepping inside the dimly lit room, he kicked the door shut and gently laid her on the bed. His eyes never left her sensuously clad body as he raised himself to a standing position and began to tear at his clothing.

She could feel the heat blazing across the short distance between them, and she smiled and stretched with feline grace, beckoning him to her side with outstretched arms, her fingers fluttering through the air in anticipation. In moments he was lying beside her, divested of all his clothes and moving against her writhing body. He began to kiss her skin, sending her temperature soaring into the stratosphere. She could feel the power of his manhood thrusting against her leg and realized this act of love would not be the slow, relaxed sort of mating she had known in his arms before. His control was being ripped to shreds, and she had to admit hers was no better.

The words he whispered in her ear increased her pulsebeat to a wild tempo. "This hot little number you're wearing is the sexiest thing I've ever seen . . . or felt." He gave a savage-sweet growl. "But if I don't find a way to get at your luscious body soon, I swear I'm going to tear it off you!" he threatened.

"It might be the fastest method," she murmured, knowing she was giving him permission to do anything he wished.

He jerked his head up to make sure he had heard her correctly. Seeing her full, warm mouth curve into a smile of understanding, he knew it was all right. "I'll buy you a dozen new ones," he promised, straddling her aroused body and pulling the red silk garment from her smooth shoulders. They laughed in relief when they heard the fragile straps snap. "Hell, I'll buy you *two* dozen, sweetheart," he corrected exuberantly. "This is fun!"

He sat across her moving legs, visually exploring her supple flesh. "My God, you're beautiful, Crissy," he breathed in a worshipful voice as he pulled the teddy and her hose from her legs. She knew the time for laughter was over. Lifting her arms to welcome his body to hers, she whispered, "I love you, darling."

His reply filled her senses with love. "You're mine," he proclaimed, the deeply resonant words torn from his chest. "You're mine . . . *forever*," he cried, entering her moist warmth possessively.

"Forever," she promised, moving against him in the timeless action of love.

He held her in his arms as if he never meant to let her go again. Thrusting smoothly and powerfully, his body became slick with a sheen of perspiration. Crissy's wondrous touch slid along his skin as she sought a closer union with the man she loved. She fastened her hold around his body with arms and her legs, moaning irrationally as she felt her hold on reality flee before the rumbling force of her passion.

She was being pushed beyond her control, if control she had ever had, and she cried out his name over and over again when her loins began their climactic, pulsating throb of release. Moments later James followed her over the edge and shuddered his pleasure at her involvement.

"I've been ravished." He chuckled, rolling to her side and bringing her with him. "I'd forgotten what a strong-willed woman you are." A satisfied smile lit his relaxed face.

"I'll never let you forget it again," she promised, snuggling against his chest and playing with the soft hair and small, flat nipples. "I love you too much to be just an interested bystander," she informed him with a giggle.

"I wouldn't want it any other way, sweetheart. You're all woman . . . and you're *my* woman, baby," he crooned, appreciatively.

They lay together, silently resting as they shared a mutual thought. "I've truly met my match," each one mused, unaware of their shared wisdom.

He moved her more comfortably against his length and spoke almost as if he were talking to himself. "We have a lot to do before we get married. Where would you like to go on our honeymoon, darling?" he asked, kissing her soft hair.

"Can't we just stay home?"

He chuckled softly. "If I'm counting correctly, we have four altogether—your cabin and apartment, my lake home and this penthouse. Which will it be, my lady?"

"Why, the lake house, where else?" she answered. "But we can spend some nights in my cabin, if you'd like."

"I'd like," he said in a low murmur, holding her close. "What about your work?"

She hoped he wouldn't become upset with what she had to tell him. "I can't leave the kids in the lurch," she explained. "They'll be counting on me for help with their speech competition. But I'll give notice that I'll be leaving at the end of the semester. Is that all right with you?"

She saw that he was frowning slightly, and steeled herself for his refusal, but he was surprisingly agreeable. "It will mean more driving for you than I'd like, but we'll work out some sort of schedule, honey. You know, I'll be very busy, too, with the Christmas rush—actually, the rush to fill the orders for the spring sales. We have to think ahead by several months," he told her.

"I know," she whispered.

He laughed again. "God, I keep forgetting that you're Belle Grady, too. You know as much as I do about sales campaigns, don't you?"

She nodded. "Is my commercial career going to be a problem, James?" she asked. "You know I love my work."

"No problem, darling," he said, comfortingly. "Just as long as Prince Toys has first dibs on your services."

"Always," she replied, knowing she'd give the company's president anything he wanted.

"Baby, in that one word, you've answered just about any other question I could ask," he said. "God, I love you."

"And I love you." She kissed him then with every bit of love in her heart, knowing she would never have to worry about any woman's designs on her husband-to-be. Her efforts to show him all that she was feeling were not wasted. He pulled her tightly into his warm, enveloping embrace. "You know, we may have to add another wing to the lake house. We'll need the extra room for the kids."

She lifted her head sleepily from his broad chest and eyed him suspiciously. "How many children do you want, Mr. Prince?"

"You're talking formally again, Ms. Brant," he reminded her, giving her bottom a pinch. Ignoring her squirming effort to escape, he went on, complacently. "Oh, I think six is a nice round number."

She thumped him playfully on his solar plexis. "Six will certainly turn *me* into a nice round number," she grumbled good-naturedly. "Why don't we just start with one," she countered, "and play it by ear from there?"

"Why don't we?" he agreed, pulling her on top of his body and beginning another erotic journey to utopia. "We've got to keep at it, though, if we're going to have our own in-house testing team," he informed her with a deadpan expression.

"Testing team?" she squeaked as he found one of her pleasure points and began to delve into its sweetness.

"For all the toys, sweetheart," he explained calmly, swinging over her soft, hot length to take control of their coming adventure.

She laughed throatily. "You have the most fascinating mind!" she murmured, feeling the throb of his manhood inside her aroused body.

His deep chuckle of pleasure vibrated in his chest. Then, explanations were no longer necessary as he covered her moaning lips with his passionate kiss.

THE EDITOR'S CORNER

It seems only a breathless moment ago that we launched LOVESWEPT into the crowded sea of romance publishing. And yet with publication of this month's titles we mark the end of LOVESWEPT'S first full year on the stands. An anniversary is a wonderful thing for many reasons . . . and not the least of them is that it prompts a little reflection about the past twelve months and the twelve months to come. As you know, we run a statement about our publishing goals for the LOVESWEPT romances in the front of each of our novels. Reviewing our books for the past year, I can't help feeling proud of the numbers of times we were able to reach the goal of providing you with a "keeper." Heartfelt bravos and gratitude to our wonderful authors and to the scores of people on the Bantam Books staff who've made this possible. Each time we've reached the goal of providing a truly fresh, creative love story, we find that our goal expands and we have a new standard of freshness and creativity to strive for. And, so, we've grown professionally and personally and will go on growing.

Each title for next month represents to us one of the overall ingredients we want in the books in our line. **TO SEE THE DAISIES . . . FIRST** symbolizes the freshness and optimism of our romances; **NO RED ROSES,** again a flower image, represents the kind of true romance of our stories; **THAT OLD FEELING,** certainly expresses our goal of providing novels that truly touch the emotions, that can sometimes make you laugh—and sometimes make you cry; and **SOME-THING DIFFERENT . . .** is the phrase that describes the highest of our goals—and the hardest to reach—to

(continued)

bring you very creative love stories full of delightful surprises. But, I bet you want me to move away from all the general talk and settle down into the specific—namely, letting you know about the four stories you have to look forward to next month.

In **TO SEE THE DAISIES . . . FIRST,** LOVESWEPT #43, Billie Green gives us another of her captivating love stories full of humor and tinged with pathos. Ben Garrison knew his life was lacking something, but he didn't know what until he met an enchanting woman who wore only a man's trenchcoat and had absolutely no idea who she was! Ben named her Sunny, because she was as life-giving as the sun's warm rays. He opened his home and his heart to her, but soon her past threatened both her and their love.

Ah, now you'll know! Mike Novacek isn't the hero of **NO RED ROSES,** as you probably realized from that broad hint we gave you in last month's Editor's Corner. Rex Brody is the hero and what an irresistible one! Iris really knows how to give us a lovable man, doesn't she? In **NO RED ROSES,** LOVESWEPT #44, heroine Tamara Ledford should have been prepared for almost anything because she'd grown up with her psychic aunt. But even her aunt couldn't fully warn her about Rex, and how the famous singer would whirl into her life and whisk her away. Tamara allowed herself to fall in love with Rex as he showered her with flowers that symbolized beauty and sensuality while she hid her hurt that he never gave her red roses, the flowers that mean love. Thanks to Iris for giving that wonderful, charming Rex the love he so richly deserved.

Remember Fayrene Preston's first LOVESWEPT #4, **SILVER MIRACLES?** From line one you could just feel that hot, sultry Texas night surrounding her characters. Here again in **THAT OLD FEELING,** LOVESWEPT #45, Fayrene is at her most sensually evocative, bringing settings and senses to full life.

Christopher Saxon wants his wife Lisa back, and follows her on vacation to Baja, California, where he convinces her that they should try again. But even as Lisa is melting in his embrace, she is worrying: for, if their love has survived their separation, have the problems that drove them apart years earlier survived, too?

Kay Hooper's LOVESWEPT #46, **SOMETHING DIFFERENT,** delivers just what the title says it will. Kay's superb originality and wit has never been shown off better than in this love story which is a delicious brew of delectable characters, both human and animal. The heroine, Gypsy Taylor, is a famous mystery writer who doesn't believe heroes exist in the modern-day world. Chase Mitchell sets out to prove her wrong. He gives her the Lone Ranger, Zorro—and himself. Some of Chase's antics are outrageous, almost as outrageous as Gypsy's piratical cat named Corsair!

As we celebrate our first year, our warmest thoughts go out to each and every loyal reader who has taken our LOVESWEPT romances off the shelves and into her heart. Cards and letters from fans along with the generous support of booksellers have made this a year full of beautiful memories. As we promised the day we started LOVESWEPT and have promised every day since—we will always try to publish love stories you'll never forget by authors you'll always remember.

Sincerely,

Carolyn Nichols

Carolyn Nichols
Editor
LOVESWEPT
Bantam Books, Inc.
666 Fifth Avenue
New York, NY 10103